Kill Your Darlings

Cat Voleur

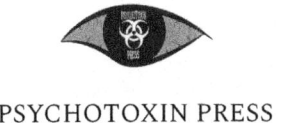

PSYCHOTOXIN PRESS

Copyright © 2023 by Cat Voleur

All rights reserved.

No part of this publication may be reproduced, distributed, or transmitted in any form or by any means, including photocopying, recording, or other electronic or mechanical methods, without the prior written permission of the publisher, except as permitted by U.S. copyright law.

The story, all names, characters, and incidents portrayed in this production are fictitious. No identification with actual persons (living or deceased), places, buildings, and products is intended or should be inferred.

Book Cover by Grim Poppy

First Printing
©2023 PsychoToxin Press

Join us or stay sane @ www.psychotoxin.com

ISBN: 9798866664986

PsychoToxin Press is Christopher Pelton, Jester Knieght, and Cat Voleur.

KILL YOUR DARLINGS

Cover design services for the beautifully creepy. Premades, customs, magazine covers, etc.

Twitter: @grimpoppydesign

Patreon: patreon.com/grimpoppydesign

Contents

Dedication		1
Introduction		2
1.	My Salt, His Wounds	5
2.	d3t0x	15
3.	The Grass Red and the Trees Dark	30
4.	Castaway	40
5.	L'Arabesque	53
6.	Enlightenment	66
7.	Imaginary, But Very Real	76
8.	You'll Just Be Nothing	83
9.	Until He Starves	95
10.	Revenge Body	103
11.	Ramen of Regret	112
12.	Twelve Hour Lifespan	115
13.	Not Like Lettie	126
14.	Revenir	141
15.	The Six Suitors of Miss Lucy Westenra	147

Story Notes	157
Acknowledgements	168
About the Author	170
Also By	171

To all those who write rejection letters, thank you.

No, seriously. Thank you.

Introduction

Dear Readers,

I cannot thank you enough for picking up this collection. All my writing is important to me, but the fifteen stories that follow are very near and dear to my heart.

They may look unrelated. They are written in different styles, they cover different themes, and feature different phases of my writing. Some of them represent my growing pains as a writer over the last couple years. This collection could appear, to an outsider, like something mashed together of nothing but the spare parts I had laying around. In fact, they have been in the works for a long time now, and are curated very carefully.

When I first conceived of the collection, the working title was *The Last Round of Consideration*. Indeed, most of the stories featured made it to the last round of consideration for *at least one* anthology before ending up back in my possession, unpublished. I was at a point in my career where my style was evolving, and even though the feedback was incredible, I found that the acceptances were drying up. I was getting shortlisted and rejected, praised and rejected, invited to submit, and subsequently rejected.

I think most writers go through phases like this. I think most *any* creative who likes to challenge themselves has a drawer full of similar projects: the ones that were too weird, or not weird enough, or just in the wrong place at the wrong time. When I was first playing with the idea of a collection, and gathering up all my pieces, these tales were still so fresh. They were indicative of my work, and I absolutely thought of them as my best. Every single time they *almost* made it in somewhere, I grew more determined to get them published somewhere else.

I weeded out and reworked the weakest ones. I employed extra beta readers. I edited. I succeeded in getting a couple of the more marketable ones published. I spent a lot of time trying to find homes for the ones that are left. I put off releasing a collection for so long because I still thought each and every one of these would find a home in an anthology or magazine. They were *so* close to making it at some of the most aspirational markets I've ever submitted to.

I spent so much time re-editing and resubmitting these that they stopped representing my voice as a writer. I have a different way of approaching fiction now than I do when I drafted them, and I hope to evoke different things in my readers than what I wanted at the time. I got out of my dry spell, and started writing new stuff, but these were my favorites. It was hard to let them go.

There's a piece of writing advice that you've probably heard. "Kill your darlings."

While I've seen plenty of writers and often film critics use this literally to refer to character deaths, what it really means is that sometimes creatives get attached to the wrong aspect of their work. Sometimes projects evolve past our original ideas for them, take on a life of their own, and become about something else. In order to take them to that next level, sometimes you have to cut out the thing that stops them from getting there, whether it's a beloved character, or a cool line of dialogue, or a subplot that doesn't matter the way you thought it did. Sometimes, they're entire works of fiction that just can't be your focus any longer than they have been.

I like to think I've grown a lot as a writer over the last couple years. My time in publishing has taught me so many things, and I am constantly inspired to be better and weirder and more prolific by the talented colleagues that I am honored to call my friends. I've changed a lot, and there are stranger, darker words waiting for me on the horizon. But I have to have the freedom to focus on them.

These fifteen tales are my rejects, and my experiments, and my growing pains. They are, simply put, my darlings.

Thank you, for helping me finally put them to rest. I could not imagine a better sendoff.

— Cat Voleur

My Salt, His Wounds

♥

"What the hell are you?" He hisses.

I recognize his voice so well that the image of him is all tangled up in the sound. I can see perfectly every horrified twist in his expression before my eyes are even open.

There is an attempt to answer, even before words have come to mind, but it is weak. I am weak. I am terrified to let the question hang in the air, and yet it does. Not only is my mind blank, but my throat is in utter agony. From the moment my mouth opens enough to let the air rush in, it burns. Everything tastes of salt. Even the idea of speaking seems intolerably cruel.

I force my eyes open and turn my face toward him, not bothering to take a look at myself beforehand. I don't attempt to take in my surroundings or search for the source of my various aches and pains. I look to him first. Always to him.

He is looming over me in the dim light of our basement. I'm curled up on the floor, craning my bruised neck to stare up in his direction. The position, like all else, hurts. It is painful to the point my body screams at me while I still cannot make a sound. Still, my efforts are met by only with silent hostility. With expectation. There is cruelty burning away in his eyes.

I'm more scared of him now than I have ever been. It's not just that I am injured, or confused, though both of these things are true. It's that I hardly recognize him as he is right now.

This is a man I've loved at his worst. A monster to whom I have so willingly bound myself. My lover's dark nature is something I am infinitely well versed in, but this is different. Wrong. His features are so contorted in anger and disgust that I almost weep to look upon him.

Almost.

Instead, I plead.

With my eyes, and heart, and soul, I beg to be forgiven for whatever crime it was he thinks I have committed. The words still will not come. I clutch my hand to my heart shakily. I feel the apology that I cannot speak. If he understands this, there is still no mercy to be found in him. He doesn't want an apology; I know. He wants an answer.

What the hell am I?

The question makes no sense. My situation makes no sense. I want to be heard, but I am denied. My anguished sob dies silently within my throat. My neck is aching, and another attempt to open my mouth fails. There is a roaring, croaking, pattering sound that I cannot explain. It pours from me in place of what he wants to hear.

He steps back.

And again.

Another step.

He runs.

I can hear his panicked footsteps stumbling up the stairs. A door slams. I can hear the lock click. There is a chair being dragged across the floor and wedged firmly under the doorknob. It is impossible, yet I can also hear his labored breathing. Still. I can hear more than that, too. The spiders weaving their webs in the basement we now share. The worms crawling in the dirt outside. I can hear everything, it seems, except my heartbeat. I can hear him, though, as though my pounding head were on his chest.

Each of my labored breaths hurt. The air coming in feels like sandpaper on my raw throat and it rubs me bloody before settling down like lead poured into my lungs. All too soon, my chest is crushed from the weight of all this oxygen.

I lay back on the ground, and beg for the darkness to reclaim me.

There is little relief when it finally does.

I was on top of him.

His face was red from screaming. My thighs were aching as they stretched over him.

The position felt so unnatural, but I hadn't been able to move.

I had been crying. The tears were still on my cheek. My eyes were burning, bulging.

His thumbs dug in tighter.

I couldn't move.

I don't know how long he keeps me down here. I sleep, and time has no meaning. I wake to find that I am never quite the version of myself that I last remember. My memories ebb away, and become dreams, and I do not always remember those either. It feels fluid, and surreal. Such is my existence now.

It feels like a long time, but I cannot be sure.

It is several sleep cycles, at least, before I find the strength to pull myself into a sitting position and lean against the wall.

What the hell are you?

That is the thing I remember most clearly from the past, those words that he spat at me before expecting an answer.

The question seems as important as it is strange. My mind gets caught on it several times before I can acknowledge any of what it means. There is a wave of relief when such enlightenment finally comes. For some reason, he is now as afraid of me as I have been of him. This gives me time to consider. It gives me hope. He ran from me. Fled. He has never done that before, and it implies that for some reason, in some unknown way, I have power.

I attain some semblance of clarity, and am able to move onto other thoughts, other facts. None of them are particularly pleasant, but they are good to know all the same.

I am in the basement. I am in immense pain. There is a monster who often paces on the floor just above me. I can still hear him. He looks like someone who I once loved. That someone wasn't good either, but was not ever so bad as this.

He keeps me down here.

I can hear the worry in his frantic breathing every time he thinks about me.

What am I indeed, that he has suddenly become so scared?

What was I before that I let it get this far?

He spoke so fondly of the house, his plans.
The eloquence of his words betrayed me.

He painted a picture so lovely that I could not resist getting lost in his vision.

A beautiful place, he had whispered softly, where we would be alone. No external stress for our love, not a single obligation for me, but him.

From the very first time he spoke of it, it felt real. *Like it could be real, anyway, like I wanted to help bring it forth into our lives.*

I was blinded by the sentiment — so blind that I could not see my prison for what it was until I was already trapped within its walls. I was so blind I believed my isolation was a desirable thing, to be sought and treasured.

I believed it would be a fairy tale, and not, as it proved, a nightmare.

I revel in my newfound clarity, though there was a time these thoughts might have easily drowned me. A single drop of these revelations would have felt heavier than I could bear. Dwelling down here, alone, I can admit I was a broken person then.

Now, *I* feel ready to do the drowning.

I believe I have the capacity for such a thing, as I did not before. There is a torrent of things within me that are waiting to be released, the things I have dammed up inside myself.

He continues to pace back and forth.

He waits.

He bides his time.

Considers.

I have time.

I have infinitely more time than him.

I wait, too.

Our screams grew louder in tandem with one another.

There was no reason, in our seclusion, to try and tamper them. Each day, he grew more restless. I grew more afraid.

Constantly, I was the one who paid the price. When he had a thing, he wanted something else. As time wore on, I could give him less and less, since he already had all of me. My wants were whittled away in favor of his. My sense of self soon followed.

I had become a thing of the past. The house was not as he had promised it would be.

Our lives were not half so pretty as the picture he had painted.

So the screaming grew; mine and his. Fear, and anger. Louder by the day.

And when he had squeezed the last sound from me, it was still not enough.

What amazes me now, as I stare up at the steps, is how it doesn't feel different.

Before, he procured my isolation through words and deeds, and the physical distance between our life and the life I had known prior to him. Now he does it with a lock, and a barricade, and darkness. I have changed, and he has changed, but this dynamic between us has remained the same through all our other transformations.

It will not be the same forever, I know.

It is well past time for equal footing.

I'm angry with myself for giving my voice away to such a heartless creature.

My blindness of before is now a raging sore of regret within me. It all looks so clear from where I sit. How could I have not seen it all before?

Before the anger can fester too much, I turn it, righteously, unto him. That is where it belongs.

I did not give my voice. He took it from me. He dried it all up with his abuse.

I am blameless.

As soon as I have acknowledged this, I feel the ache in my body begin to ease. I have the capacity to drown, yes, but also the capacity to forgive. That was a gift I always had before, and one that I used so foolishly to overlook all his discretions. I turn this forgiveness upon myself for the first time. This is where it belongs.

The basement no longer feels so cold. My rage, when directed properly, is a warm pool all around me. I cannot tell where my skin ends and my oasis begins.

I bring up more memories of him, that I might flood the world around me.

The meat of his palm across my face.
The sting.
The violence.
The ringing of my ears as I failed to breathe.
His thumbnails scrape my skin, his digits crushed my connection to his world once and for all.

I thought he would release me. I thought I was safe from the end as we pushed closer and closer to the edge.

He had never taken it this far before.

Never.

I thought he never would.

He didn't.

Until he did.

It only took that one time.

The pacing stops.

Not for the night. Not for a break. I can hear the definitive nature of it. I hear the sound of the chair scraping once more, and know that he has finally decided to come down.

I stand to meet him.

The lock turns.

I feel surprisingly buoyant.

The door opens.

An amazing thing has happened in the darkness. I have forgotten the man so much that the monster before me seems little more than air. He is nothing but a breeze that recoils when it takes in the sight of me.

There is salvation to be found here. My heart soars. The only weight left is the air still lodged in my lungs from before. It sits heavily in me, a final reminder of my last attempt to be his wife. My last inclination to ever cower before him.

A gun trembles in his weak hands. What would have once terrified me now means nothing. The metal is as flimsy and as gaseous as the creature wielding it.

His voice is hardly there at all, little more than a breath. Again, he asks me that question.

"What the hell are you?"

I am smiling. I am strong. I am fierce, and wild, and infinite. I can see all of that now, which I could not before. What I don't see is any reason why I should answer to him.

This new freedom, like his fear, is intoxicating.

"You should be dead," he whispers into the long silence. There is so much I cannot read in the tone of this stranger, this thing on the stairs above me. I would have been happy to bask in his discomfort forever, but this gets my attention.

Did you kill me?

I think the question as I try to recall that which my vengeance has cleansed from my memory. The answer is swirling somewhere around me, in my private sea, but it hardly seems to matter now.

I don't know if he can somehow hear my thoughts, but his face makes it clear that he has picked up on the tone of my accusation.

"It was an accident."

Too little, too late.

"Goddamn it Mikaela, it was an accident!"

Was that my name? Before?

I don't remember.

It must have been, though I have little connection to it now. I am not the person I was. I have evolved past all that.

I've evolved past a need for you.

He covers his ears, slamming the metal into the side of his own head in the desperate act. He looks miserable and pained.

"Would you shut the hell up?" He screams.

I smile to know that he cannot silence me this time.

My thoughts are now as loud to him as his stares once felt to me. Powerful. Thunderous. All-consuming.

I want to give him a better taste. I think at him. I think loudly.

I do not even need words, just the pent up emotion of all those years. The floodgates open.

He points the gun at me, his hands shaking and blood leaking from his ears.

He shoots at me, where he thinks my chest must be.

He thought he killed me once before and tried to starve me out once after. This mortal weapon is no more effective than his previous two attempts to ensure my destruction.

All the same, he needs to be taught.

He must learn that I am not a thing to be hurt. Not an outlet for his rage. Not anymore, not ever.

So I force the remaining air from my body into one, final scream.

I brace myself for a pain that does not come. The release is soothing, and cool. With the last traces of dryness gone from my body, I become weightless.

The monster before me is torn to shreds by the sound.

I look down at the bloody form, and from its shredded lips, the question emerges for a final time.

"What...are...you...?"

I wash over him, my salt flooding his wounds. It is more than he deserves.

After all, the ocean need not answer to anyone.

d3t0x

♥

Date: Thursday, December 7th, 2023 at 4:55pm (PST)
From: Melanie Wilson <MEWilson15@d3t0x.com>
To: Ada <HR@d3tox.com>
Subject: A Couple Concerns

Ada,

Thank you so much again for your help with the presentation on Monday. I think it went really well! People seem quite responsive to the new campaign.

I do have just a couple concerns regarding this new push.

As you know, I don't have the clearance to address these issues with development directly, and I was wondering if you could get me a meeting with them or with management? I think it's something we really want to talk about before taking this next step as a company.

Sincerely,

Mel

Date: Thursday, December 7th, 2023 at 4:57pm (PST)
From: Ada <HR@d3tox.com>
To: Melanie Wilson <MEWilson15@d3t0x.com>
Subject: Re: A Couple Concerns

Mel,

No problem at all! You know we're all one big family here at d3t0x.

Maybe you could tell me what these concerns are, and I can bring them up with management personally? You know we're on a tight schedule for this next update.

All the best,
Ada

Date: Thursday, December 7th, 2023 at 5:17 pm (PST)
From: Melanie Wilson <MEWilson15@d3t0x.com>
To: Ada <HR@d3tox.com>
Subject: Re: A Couple Concerns

Ada,

Thank you for getting to my email so fast! I know you're busy.

My main concern is just about the branding. I think the app's tagline is very eye-catching, but I don't know if it's wise to keep it moving forward. I feel like it sends messages that are not in line with our mission here. We're trying to do good. We're not trying to incentivize people to cut ties with their friends and family.

I've been working on a couple other options I think may be suitable. I know I'm not in development, but a softer tagline could mean softer social media campaigns. I think that's what we need after last week's controversy.

There have also been some concerns in the forums recently regarding the overall impact that this is having on people's offline relationships. Obviously, that's going to happen once in a while. I don't know if there's anything we could do to soften those blows, but I'm sure our users would take comfort in knowing that we've heard their concerns and are looking into it.

I actually tried to bring that up on Monday, but I got the feeling that you didn't think it was the time or place. I'm sorry if it was an inappropriate conversation to broach in front of the shareholders.

Thank you again,

-Mel

Date: Thursday, December 7th, 2023 at 5:18pm (PST)
From: Ada <HR@d3tox.com>
To: Melanie Wilson <MEWilson15@d3t0x.com>
Subject: Re: A Couple Concerns

Melanie,

Who could you afford to live without?

Date: Thursday, December 7th, 2023 at 5:38 pm (PST)
From: Melanie Wilson <MEWilson15@d3t0x.com>
To: Ada <HR@d3tox.com>
Subject: Re: A Couple Concerns

Ada,

Yes. That is the tagline I was referring to. It served to bring users in when we got started, but I think it's a little aggressive for the image we're now trying to maintain.

-Mel.

Date: Thursday, December 7th, 2023 at 5:42pm (PST)
From: Ada <HR@d3tox.com>

To: Melanie Wilson <MEWilson15@d3t0x.com>
Subject: Re: A Couple Concerns

Melanie,

I meant it. Who could you live without?

Date: Thursday, December 7th, 2023 at 5:50 pm (PST)
From: Melanie Wilson <MEWilson15@d3t0x.com>
To: Ada <HR@d3tox.com>
Subject: Re: A Couple Concerns

Ada,

I'm not sure what you're asking me exactly. I love and am very close to the people in my life right now. I don't want to cut any ties — and I know the company doesn't want that either.

This is a charity, a social experiment. It's not meant to drive a wedge. Right?

As you know, I got this job because I was one of the first 100 users of the original app. I believe in what we're doing. I've used the flagging system as directed, and I always go over the quarterly reports to see which of my acquaintances are costing me the most money through the micro-donations that I've signed up for. It's led me to have some difficult conversations with my family and myself, but I don't intend to actually cut anyone from my life.

That's not what this is.

I can't afford to lose anyone. I'm sure you feel the same about the people in your own life.

-Mel

Date: Thursday, December 7th, 2023 at 6:01pm (PST)
From: Ada <HR@d3tox.com>
To: Melanie Wilson <MEWilson15@d3t0x.com>
Subject: Re: A Couple Concerns

Mel,

I believe you.

You're sitting at your desk emailing me about this an hour after you were free to leave. On a Thursday night, when we expect you in early tomorrow, no less.

I don't believe you believe you can afford to lose a single person in your life right now.

Did you know that you use our micro donation system more than any other employee?

Did you know I could see that?

Date: Thursday, December 7th, 2023 at 6:19 pm (PST)
From: Melanie Wilson <MEWilson15@d3t0x.com>
To: Ada <HR@d3tox.com>
Subject: Re: A Couple Concerns

Ada,

I'm not sure that I appreciate the direction this conversation is going.

Surely if you have access to the financial information of the people at the company, and what they're spending on the app, you should also know that it's private.

As to your insinuation that I don't have better things to do, I hoped you would take it as a sign I care about this company. Not as a sign of my personal obligations.

Please tell management my concerns.

-Mel

Date: Thursday, December 7th, 2023 at 6:19pm (PST)
From: Ada <HR@d3tox.com>
To: Melanie Wilson <MEWilson15@d3t0x.com>

Subject: Re: A Couple Concerns

Did you know that your family is beginning to drop you from their circles?

Date: Thursday, December 7th, 2023 at 6:24pm (PST)
From: Ada <HR@d3tox.com>
To: Melanie Wilson <MEWilson15@d3t0x.com>
Subject: Re: A Couple Concerns

Of course you did.

That's why you brought this up with me.

There have always been doubts in the forums. We've been making waves since we launched the beta version in May.

Didn't you know that the outrage brings the money in? Didn't you wonder how we've been developing so fast?

You're not concerned about the tagline because you think it will go against our charitable image. You're worried that you've been using the app wrong. People are starting to get rid of *you* before you get rid of *them*.

You're the outcast.

You just can't stand that, can you?

Date: Thursday, December 7th, 2023 at 6:34pm (PST)
From: Ada <HR@d3tox.com>
To: Melanie Wilson <MEWilson15@d3t0x.com>
Subject: Re: A Couple Concerns

I know you're at your desk, Mel.

I can see that you're still clocked in.

Date: Thursday, December 7th, 2023 at 6:19 pm (PST)
From: Melanie Wilson <MEWilson15@d3t0x.com>
To: Ada <HR@d3tox.com>
Subject: Re: A Couple Concerns

I don't understand why you're being like this.

Date: Thursday, December 7th, 2023 at 6:34pm (PST)
From: Ada <HR@d3tox.com>
To: Melanie Wilson <MEWilson15@d3t0x.com>
Subject: Re: A Couple Concerns

We're family, Mel.

This is called tough love.

You knew what we were. A charity project meets social experiment.

You helped us grow.

You helped make us.

You should accept us.

Date: Thursday, December 7th, 2023 at 6:39 pm (PST)
From: Melanie Wilson <MEWilson15@d3t0x.com>
To: Ada <HR@d3tox.com>
Subject: Re: A Couple Concerns

Exactly Ada!

We're a charity project!

We've done so much good. You said it yourself; I spend more on this damned app than anyone here. It's thanks to d3t0x that I've been able to put money towards causes I care in when the social climate seems to care about them least.

I'm putting good back into the world.

I don't understand why you're treating me this way.

I only wanted to help.

Date: Thursday, December 7th, 2023 at 6:41pm (PST)
From: Ada <HR@d3tox.com>
To: Melanie Wilson <MEWilson15@d3t0x.com>
Subject: Re: A Couple Concerns

You forgot the part about the social experiment, Mel.

We wanted to see how people would react. We wanted to see who they could afford to live without.

There are so many sites to connect people. So many ways to bring in toxicity. We're just trying to clean a bit of that up.

Date: Thursday, December 7th, 2023 at 6:44 pm (PST)
From: Melanie Wilson <MEWilson15@d3t0x.com>
To: Ada <HR@d3tox.com>
Subject: Re: A Couple Concerns

You wanted this from the start, didn't you?

To solidify echo chambers?

To drive people apart while taking some of the profit?

Is that what you've been the whole time?

Date: Thursday, December 7th, 2023 at 6:52pm (PST)
From: Ada <HR@d3tox.com>
To: Melanie Wilson <MEWilson15@d3t0x.com>
Subject: Re: A Couple Concerns

We just wanted to see what would happen.

Now we have.

But you're an anomaly, Mel.

You just keep feeding the machine, plodding along, never learning. You don't represent what the people want, only what they *pretend* to want. I think it's long overdue that we get on the same page.

You need to delete someone.

Date: Thursday, December 7th, 2023 at 6:53 pm (PST)
From: Melanie Wilson <MEWilson15@d3t0x.com>
To: Ada <HR@d3tox.com>
Subject: Re: A Couple Concerns

No. I don't.

Date: Thursday, December 7th, 2023 at 6:56pm (PST)
From: Ada <HR@d3tox.com>
To: Melanie Wilson <MEWilson15@d3t0x.com>
Subject: Re: A Couple Concerns

You'll lose them anyway.

They can afford to live without you.

But you can't afford to live without us.

Delete someone.

Just one person.

Anyone.

Date: Thursday, December 7th, 2023 at 6:59pm (PST)
From: Ada <HR@d3tox.com>
To: Melanie Wilson <MEWilson15@d3t0x.com>
Subject: Re: A Couple Concerns

Your uncle Jim, maybe?

He costs you an awful lot with those trophy hunting photos. You were very against those when you filled out the survey. Can you really tell me he's a positive influence in your life?

Or what about Carol Stevens from college?

You're costing her a pretty penny every time you post a vegan recipe you know, she may be about to delete you anyway.

You don't need as many of these people as you think you do. I'm just trying to help.

Date: Thursday, December 7th, 2023 at 7:12pm (PST)
From: Ada <HR@d3tox.com>
To: Melanie Wilson <MEWilson15@d3t0x.com>
Subject: Re: A Couple Concerns

Good girl.

Interesting choice.

I'll see you back at work on Monday, bright and early, alright?

I think you're going to do well here.

Date: Thursday, December 7th, 2023 at 7:13 pm (PST)
From: Melanie Wilson <MEWilson15@d3t0x.com>
To: Ada <HR@d3tox.com>
Subject: Re: A Couple Concerns

Monday?

Date: Thursday, December 7th, 2023 at 6:52pm (PST)
From: Ada <HR@d3tox.com>
To: Melanie Wilson <MEWilson15@d3t0x.com>
Subject: Re: A Couple Concerns

Take tomorrow off.

You need the long weekend to think about your future here, and who you can afford to live without.

The Grass Red and the Trees Dark

♥

Keira had abandoned something truly magical back in the woods. As she approached the ramshackle old house from the tree line, and not from the gravel path, she had to wonder why she was returning at all.

There's nothing for me here.

She stopped walking when the blue light of the old TV came into view, the sound of it blaring through the busted out window. It cast a pale and inconsistent glow onto the trash around the property, putting into prominence the cigarette butts and rusted beer cans that lay where her mother had once grown herbs.

It had been for the sake of her mother's memory that Keira had returned, and that was all. A ghost can only hold control for so long.

There is nothing for me here, she thought again.

Keira considered her options from a safe distance.

She could always enter the house. That would most likely lead to a nasty confrontation with her father. He'd demand to know what had kept her out late, where she had been, why she didn't call, and if he were in a particularly foul mood, who she was fucking. She hated the vulgarity of the question more each time he asked. Even worse was the hypocrisy. Growing up, she wouldn't have been allowed to say so much as the word 'heck' without a beating. She didn't doubt he'd try to take the belt to her even now if she threw his favorite profanity back at him.

Another route would be to sneak in, as she often had, through the window of her bedroom. Of course, experience taught her the risk of getting caught. It hardly seemed worth the chance for the cheap reward of a greasy, microwavable dinner — even the thought of which was enough to churn her stomach.

"I could go back to the fairy circle."

The thought came to her unbidden, as though being whispered in her ear. She was almost certain she had not been the one to think it, but a quick glance around confirmed she was alone.

This solution seemed so plausible that it took her breath away. She could go back to the circle, and more than that, she *wanted* to. It would be as easy as turning around.

Instead, she walked around the dilapidated building in a wide circle, heading for the backyard before she could give the idea more thought. If she thought about it too much, she'd find herself back there in the field of mushrooms, and that was something too dangerous to consider.

Keira hoped she would not be as susceptible to the desire once she was in her own small place of power; her tree house.

The boards creaked and groaned under her weight as she climbed up, but she had faith they would hold. Her safe haven had once been built for two, after all.

The floral murals waiting for her on the walls were familiar enough as to get her mind off her troubles as she went through the motions of preparing herself for the night. She closed the trapdoor beneath her and locked it by way of jamming a small twig into the crack. It did virtually nothing, but it was a well-established ritual from her childhood that she dare not break now. "Locking the doors will keep the monsters out," her mother had told her once. Tonight, she was just hoping that locking the door could keep her in.

If anything could fight the beauty of what she had seen, it would be the comfort of the one place she might actually miss — the one place where she had ever felt truly safe.

She grabbed the rolled up sleeping back from where it was stashed in the corner and unfurled it across the floor. On chilly nights she would zip herself inside, but in the warm autumn days like this she could get away with sleeping atop the padded fabric. That was always her favorite way to do things. The sleeping bag was so wide when opened, and her space so small, that the edges of the lavender flannel lining would bunch up at the corners of the room until it felt like the treehouse itself was hugging her.

Still, it would take more than a hug to drown out the siren's song that came from the forest. It was damn near consuming her as she dropped her bag and lay down in her little nest.

Maybe mom was right all along.

Margaret Byrne had been a superstitious woman to the end, and leery of the woods they lived by. She'd believed there were banshees and changelings and even demons running amok through the branches, waiting to lure small children away from their parents.

Keira had grown up hearing damn near every spooky legend that there was, and it had never made her love the trees less. Still, she'd been bound to her mother's rituals out of love and habit, if not a belief in the monsters claimed to lurk in every shadow. Throwing spilt salt over her shoulder had been one thing, even fun at times. Avoiding the forest had been another thing altogether, when she had loved it so deeply. That rule had proven over the years to be a constant test of the child's loyalty.

"I know how hard it was for you to stay away."

Margaret's voice was not a memory then, not a phantom in her own mind. It was a whisper beside her in the darkness, and it sent a shiver down Keira's spine.

Mom? She wondered, as she dared not speak aloud at first. She could hear the wind whistle through the trees at a distance, and the pounding of her own heart. "Mother?" She asked softly.

There was no answer. Keira could almost believe that she had imagined the voice, but the whole day had been so surreal that nothing seemed impossible anymore. Even in her favorite, most grounded place, nothing felt the same after seeing the mushrooms.

Her promise had only been that she would refrain from venturing into the woods alone, but that was as good as never going when her mother would so often balk at the tree line and her father would refuse to take her.

Still, she had passed the trial for a time, subsisting as best she could on their weekly walks. She had not upheld the vow for more than a week after Margaret's funeral, nearly three years past.

The child was grown now, to nineteen years of age. She was old enough to flee her father's house, and stubborn enough not to. She survived these days by spending more and more of her time in those magical woods that her mother had so feared. Never had she stopped to consider that they were anything but the escape that she so desperately needed.

"What would you call this, if not an invitation to escape?"

There was the voice again, and it did not belong to Keira's mother.

Margaret's voice had lilted lyrically with the last soft traces of an accent, but it was not the pure melodic tones of whatever was now speaking, practically singing to her. Now that she focused on it, she was unsure how she ever could have confused the two.

The silence was pressuring her to answer, and so she did.

"I'd call it a fairy ring."

The laughing at her response was all around her, and it was music.

Truly, it was the most beautiful sound she'd ever heard, and she struggled to recall why it seemed so familiar to her.

It had been fainter then, as if carried on the breeze, but it had been the same sound as the mushrooms made when she stood outside their circle — those beautiful white mushrooms.

They had stood so drastically apart from any flora that she'd ever seen in those woods. She'd taken her usual shortcut to the heart of the forest before treading the same path back through the clearing. Having traveled the same route both ways, she was certain there had not been any fungi when she'd been through at noon. Yet there they were in the evening light, their brilliant round caps reflecting the moonlight so perfectly that they seemed to glow. Their stems were marbled with pink veins that seemed to fade into the deep purple of the twilight grass.

"Don't ever step in the fairy rings."

How many times had she heard that as a child? How often had she dutifully checked to make sure that her steps did not make contact with any mushrooms — if only to show her mother that she was capable of being trusted? That had always been her motive, more than the fear that had been impossible to instill in her.

"They'll take you away to another world," Margaret had threatened. "You won't be able to come back to me."

What her mother had failed to grasp was that being swept away from her life was hardly a threat. Even back then, Keira had longed for nothing more than to be taken away to another world. To live in the woods eternal and never have to experience the boredom or loneliness or longing of their shared existence. Margaret, who also lived in that house, and with her husband, should have understood better than anyone that to be away was not a frightening prospect.

Who wants the mundane when the magical is right there?

"Fairies," her mother had tried to explain to her, "aren't just little humans with wings. There's no understanding them. They set aside all work for favor of play and intolerance of rules. To be in their realm is to give up all that makes us human."

Again, it was enticing.

"It's spoiled them!" Huffed an exasperated Margaret, who knew her child would then dream of eternal play in the forest. She'd scrambled then, though her honest soul would not allow more than new metaphors to describe what she already believed to be true. "Like how constant sweetness can rot a tooth. Constant play has spoiled them rotten."

Even back then, there was doubt in Keira as to whether or not she'd actually mind being rotten.

"You couldn't come back to me," was always the fallback.

"Then you could come with me!" Keira had yelped back in excitement over her bright plan. "You could come dance with me and the fairies and we could play together forever!"

"It isn't just that you couldn't come back." Margaret had pulled Keira onto her lap and spoken to her with such gentle sincerity. Someone else witnessing the scene might have thought they were having a conversation about death, or loss, a somber yet factual world discussion. That was how seriously her mother took such things. "It's that you wouldn't *remember* to come back to me, nor I you. We could be there, right next to each other, and we wouldn't know it. We wouldn't be ourselves. We wouldn't have our memories, the things that made us…us."

That was as close as Keira had ever gotten to being afraid of the fairies. She knew even as a child she would miss her mother.

The young woman who was witnessing true magic for the first time, however, had already been missing her mother for three years. It was only love for the memory, and habit, that made her consider going back to her father's house.

That terrible little shack of a house held no appeal, and so she had tried to think of returning somewhere more appealing; the treehouse. She'd imagined climbing up and completing her rituals to make it safe, and what it would sound like to hear her mother's voice.

"Run," it whispered. And then again "run!"

She stumbled back from it and was surprised to find that she had not actually returned to the house or the treehouse. She had not gone back to her father's property at all. There was no twig lock protecting her. She was not being hugged.

It had all seemed so terribly vivid, this vision of going back, of seeing what was waiting for her. She was almost relieved to find herself still in the clearing with the mushrooms and that wind chime laughter echoing all around.

Her body may not have traveled back, but the time was most certainly lost. The full moon had begun to sink in the sky during her vision, and the mushrooms glowed a dusty lavender rather than the pure white of earlier. The color reminded her of a certain sleeping bag that had once cradled her. She longed to be held like that again, by the very earth itself.

"Keira," whispered a spirit, but the girl was already closing her eyes to let the childlike wonder take her once more. She was preparing to jump.

The last three years had not been kind to her, and she had little enough to lose by choosing magic for a change. There were now more days she wished to forget than dreams she hoped to remember.

"I'm sorry, mom," Keira whispered, but she didn't give the ghost a chance to reply before soaring into the circle.

The leap became a twirl, a spin, and a resounding laugh. Without even opening her eyes, she felt lighter, and rejoiced to feel the burdens of the human world slip away.

The moisture of the field was warm and comforting, the ground silky soft beneath her feet as she danced along to the music. Her motions seemed the most natural thing in the world, and she couldn't remember the last time she'd let herself go like this, the last time she had been so free.

She couldn't remember much of anything.

But it was enough to feel the fairies all around her.

It must be them, for they spun and danced in time with her own body, their heartbeats thumping through them and into the very ground, existing as one to complete the ethereal song. She could hear it now in all its glory, a complex lullaby that was interrupted only by the occasional cracking of twigs underfoot.

Round and round they went, and the young creature didn't need her eyes to guide her through the sacred track in the well-worn ground. Freed spirits such as herself must have danced there for ages, and nothing could have made her happier than the knowledge she was now a part of that tradition.

Never had she felt such ecstasy, nor dreamed that the simple swaying of her body could bring about such pure bliss.

It could have been a minute or a day before she thought to slow down just a little. It was another sliver of this same timeless eternity before she felt ready at last for her eyes to feast upon the wonders that her form had acclimated to.

The light source came from all around, like fireflies, or embers that set the world aglow and lit up the most unexpected scene.

The dark trees twisted up to a deep sky, pulsing in time to the dance, curving in at the top as though to grasp the entire clearing in a domineering hand. Their twisted roots stood out starkly against the bright red grass.

What surprised her most, however, were the other dancers. They weren't fairies at all. They looked human, some form of it, and yet entirely apart from all that was familiar. Each of them moved sluggishly, with looks of terror and pain scribed across their gaunt faces.

Some looked as though they were trying to scream, their teeth bared into the fixated smiles that would not — could not — be broken.

She attributed this queer pain to the bloodied feet and broken limbs, to those who danced with jilted angles and fractured gestures. Their laughter in the music was intertwined with sobs.

For the others, she could not fathom what would scare them so. A quick glance at her own feet confirmed that she too was covered in blood up to her calf. It did not seem so terribly frightening as to cause all this fuss. It did not seem so painful, and she was confused until another wave of understanding came.

The blood was not her own. Another rotation made that obvious. The twigs snapping had not been twigs at all, but bone.

Both sides of their well-worn circle were littered with bodies of those who had fallen before their track had worn down right through them. They had been stamped back down repeatedly by the feet of all those dancers, their blood staining the grass red and the trees dark.

In the center of the field, where they could no longer move in time, the bodies writhed, still living, their moans a sweet song to which the rest of them may dance. It was as rare a beauty as the mushrooms sprouting from the damp mess of flesh.

She laughed in delight, she who no longer had a name of her own. Though she could not remember the words or warning from another life, she laid some long forgotten fear to rest about the fairies.

They could not be malevolent if they could give her this.

She had never imagined anything could be so wonderful.

Castaway

♥

THE SEA WAS GRAY, its waters rising with the storm. The winds whipped salt and sand all around the small island. A man lay, face down, still half submerged in the beach.

She ran to him.

It was time for lockdown. It was *past* time for lockdown. If the property took any damage, there would be hell to pay for it. A dead body, she thought, would not be any better, and so she pressed forward with all of her good intentions. She prayed it was not too late for him.

"Sir?" She called, still making her way over. "Hello sir? Are you alright?"

It took longer than she would have liked to reach him. The weather was cruel. Her body was not as young as it had once been. It did not move smoothly through the torrent, or across the damp ground. The edges of the water creeped in. It was not quick, but she made it to him. Still, he did not answer.

Again, she prayed.

"Hello, Sir?"

She grabbed him by the soaked shoulders of his wet suit and rolled him onto his back. She was braced for the worst, gore, the gaping flesh of a crab wound, the stench of bloat. She nearly jumped out of her skin anyway, to see what was there. His eyes were open. He spoke.

"You're not real."

She staggered back and barely avoided falling into the sand. It was a minute before she had regained enough control of her breath to speak, and another before she had any notion of what she wanted to say.

He'd said she was not real.

Her interactions with people on the island were limited enough — staff only — but she didn't think that was a normal thing for him to have said.

"Are you alright?" She asked again.

"You're not real."

The first time, she might have chalked it up to her poor hearing, or the drenched man being confused. This time, however, she could see he was awake, and alert, and she felt she had to at least try to address the accusation.

"Of course I'm real."

He did not argue this time and did not answer when she posed her myriad of questions to him.

"Who are you?"

"How did you get here?"

"Are you alright?"

They were ignored. It was only the one statement from him. He had posed it twice, initially, and then once more when she got him into view of the house. "You're not real."

There was a pause.

"This isn't real."

She could not blame him for that reaction to the estate. She'd had a rather similar feeling when she had first laid eyes on it as well. That sort of wealth could be hard to believe, and harder still to comprehend. Her disbelief, however, had not been as literal as she thought the stranger's probably was.

The best she could figure was that it was some sort of shock. She had read, or heard somewhere, that sometimes people stopped making sense when they had been through something traumatic. It was bold to assume trauma for a stranger, but he had been washed along a very private, very exclusive shore. Surely things had not been going well for him. Besides, the belief set her at ease about his behavior, and made her more confident in what she was about to do.

Her next step would have to be the same no matter, because there was only one thing that needed done. She had to get him inside. The winds were getting nastier by the minute, the sea line had followed them up the island, and the house was still exposed.

She couldn't lose this job.

She couldn't afford to pay for any property damage if something bad happened on her watch because she had failed to follow protocol.

So it was disheartening when he stopped walking, his pace slowing to a crawl before ceasing altogether, about ten feet from the door. She hoped that even if he would not converse with her, and was not in a state to answer her questions, he might still understand.

"We've got to get inside."

He squinted at her.

"Inside," she repeated.

He touched the door after a few more tentative steps.

She had the sudden urge to just push him in and be done with it, but of course she didn't.

"Listen," she said, and prayed that he would. "The storm is getting worse. And it's my job to lock up the house. So we really need to get inside, okay?"

KILL YOUR DARLINGS

It sparked something in the man. He looked to her wish fresh, surprised eyes. "Your...job?"

"Yes."

"You have a job?"

"Yes."

She did not need to tell him that he was, even now, keeping her from doing that job. He seemed to understand her irritation and impatience all on his own.

"Just one more question," he promised.

"Alright."

"What's your name?"

She wanted to look out for the man. She wanted to slap him a little bit, as well. When she had asked him his name, he had told her she wasn't real, and now he wanted to do small talk. Now? She had to take a breath and remind herself that he might have been in shock, he might have been traumatized, and in a best-case scenario he was still a castaway. The poor dear.

"Stella."

He looked surprised, and then skeptical.

"That was my mother's best friend's name in high school."

"Please?" She gestured to the door.

He relented and stepped inside.

"Let me just lock up," she told him. "Then I'll come back and we'll get you sorted out."

"You'll really come back?"

"Yes."

"Wait." He paused.

She gave him her best, stern look.

"You said you work here?"

Shock or no, her sympathy would only extend her patience so far.

"Yes."

"Alone?"

"What?"

"Do you work here alone?"

"No."

"What are the names of the others?"

"Well, there's—"

"And where are they?"

She had been prepared to play along, but then he had interrupted her. It had reminded her that this was not the time. "Will you let me go lock up, please? We can talk about—"

"It's important."

She could see the desperation in his eyes, almost akin to panic. She figured she must be going soft.

"There's Nellie. She helps me with the housekeeping, she'll be inside upstairs somewhere."

"Nellie," he said.

"There's Doug. He works on the electronics. Keeps the power running."

"Doug."

"There's Sheila, in the kitchen."

'Sheila, got it."

"And Anita."

"Anita. Where does she work?"

Stella paused.

"Where is Anita?"

"She's...gone."

He looked, strangely, relieved. He did not ask for clarification on the word gone.

"And who do you work for?"

"Mr. Wade."

The relief faltered, but only for a moment. "Nellie, Doug, Sheila, Anita, and Mr. Wade. Got it."

"Can I go?"

"Yes. I'll just think about those when you're gone."

She could hear him repeating the names to himself even as she went about her business.

"Nellie. Doug. Sheila. Anita. Mr. Wade."

He certainly was a strange man.

Shock, she told herself, but she wondered if there might not be something deeper that was wrong with him. It was not the sort of assumption she liked to make about a person, but she could not help the thought.

His whispers seemed to follow her through the house, but at least he was inside. At least she could lock up.

She didn't like what she was seeing from the windows as she went from room to room.

The world outside was losing its color to the clouds and the sea alike, threatening to turn the entire landscape into nothing but murky gray.

The view was even more alarming from upstairs.

Stella had been doing the job long enough to know it always looked worse than it was. The angle of the building always made the water look closer than it should have been. But this was different. It seemed *much* closer. She could not differentiate the sea from sky, or see a speck of sand with the way it all swirled. The island must have shrunk.

Morbid fascination held her captive longer than it should have. She might have stayed forever if there was not something else for her to do.

She needed to finish locking up.

And there was the man.

She latched the window, completing the upstairs circuit. She was careful not to take in any other views on the way back. Stella could not trust herself not to become lost.

"Nellie. Doug. Sheila. Anita. Mr. Wade." He was still whispering, standing in the entry hall where she had left him.

She could not remember leaving him there. It had been her intention to bring him in, set him in the dining area, and part of her believed that had been done. In her panic, she must not have gotten past the intention to do it.

It made her feel like a poor hostess, and a most careless rescuer. But the storm. The sea. She'd had to look out for the house.

Already she could hear it creaking in a way it had never done.

"Why don't you come sit?" She asked. "Can I get you some water?"

He followed her across the hardwood floors, dripping. Had he been dripping so much when she'd first brought him in?

Stella could not remember.

They left a trail behind them on their way into the dining room.

He didn't resist when she pulled out a chair for him, or gently pressed him into it. But he did look crazy, almost manic at the notion of water.

"Or some food?"

He glared at her.

"I had a great Aunt Nell, you know."

"Alright."

"And growing up, my neighbor had a dog named Doug. Dougie, we called him."

"I'll just be right back with that food."

Delirious, she thought. That would make sense. Lord only knew how long he had layed out in the sun for, half buried in those waves.

Anyone stuck in those conditions may well feel compelled to go a little mad.

"Sheila," she heard him mutter as she stepped into the kitchen. "Anita. Mr. Wade."

She came back with a sandwich. She set it on the table before him.

"Sheila," he said. "Mr. Wade."

She retreated to the kitchen again, and more cautiously appeared with a glass of water. He fell silent and stared at it like a madman.

"Are you trying to kill me?" He asked. His tone didn't match his face, for it did not carry his anger. It sounded raspy, and dry, and tired.

"I think you might be dehydrated."

"The seawater will not help."

"It's from the filter."

He laughed.

It was a sound of dry wood splintering against itself. It crackled in a moisture-less throat. But then he looked to the glass. He looked to Stella. He looked resigned. He drank.

Long and deep, he drank, and the glass was empty when he set it down.

Dehydrated, she thought. *Definitely.*

She went to get him another glass, which he sipped at with more caution.

His lips looked pale and bloody. The bags under his eyes seemed to darken.

"Did Sheila make this?"

"What?"

He nodded to the sandwich.

"No."

"I thought she was the cook."

"A sandwich doesn't need cooked."

"But you did see her in there? In the kitchen?"

She paused.

He waited expectantly.

"Of course," she said. "She was in the kitchen."

"Where you made the sandwich?"

"Yes."

"Did you talk to her?"

"A little."

"Does she know I'm here?"

Stella did not know what to say to that. He seemed to jump on her uncertainty.

"Can I meet her?"

"I think you'd better eat your sandwich."

He picked it up and looked it over. "What kind is it?"

"Ham."

"Where does the ham come from? Where do you get ham on an island like this?"

"Supplies are shipped in."

"For Mr. Wade?:

"Yes," she said. "And for us, working here."

"I don't know an Anita," he said.

A chill went through her. She didn't enjoy talking about Anita.

"I had wondered why there was one name I couldn't track down to anything. Is it a coincidence she's the one who's gone? But then why bother at all?"

"I think you'd better eat your sandwich."

"Ham is my favorite."

"Eat it, then."

She could not help but wonder what sort of man she had let into the house, into Mr. Wade's house. The longer they spoke, the more palpable her discomfort became. It got to the point she could barely stand it.

He did not so much as eat the sandwich as tear into it, chewing and chewing with a mad look on his face, his chapped lips growing more red.

"Anita is gone?" He asked.

"Yes."

"Dead?"

"Missing."

"They are all missing."

"What?"

"Can I meet them?"

It was not a bad idea.

She wanted very much not to be alone with the castaway anymore. Leaving the room, getting another person involved, it would put her at a greater ease. She could not help but notice how much more haggard he was looking than when he had sat down, and she had no desire to continue watching him.

"Finish your food," she said. "I'll go get Doug."

"Why not Sheila?" He asked. "Isn't the kitchen right there?"

Stella turned. She looked at the doorway. She knew Sheila was on the other side. It was time to be preparing dinner. They had talked. She was almost sure of it.

"She's busy."

"Doug then," he said.

She was relieved. Doug was not exactly what she would call a strong man, but she thought he could still overpower the stranger if need be. She scurried off to the basement, nearly slipping on the water on her way through.

"Doug?" She called. "Doug?"

The basement was finished, and usually stayed warm. But there was a chill that day which bordered on damp as she descended the stairs.

He was not there.

It was strange, because he was always there. Even when he was not in the room with the breakers, which he used as a makeshift studio to tinker with things, he preferred the basement. He had a fondness for the rec room. She practically had to drag him upstairs on cleaning days so it could be aired out.

"Doug?" She called again, but of course it did no good.

He was simply not there.

Water was trickling down the steps as she ascended them. The rising panic in her chest was stopped only by her surprise as she reached the top. It was pitch black. The windows had gone dark.

Days were long on the island. The sun would not be setting for some time yet.

But it was dark all the same.

"Doug?" She called again. "Nellie?"

"Can't find them?" Asked the castaway.

He sounded smug. Ominous.

She walked back toward the dining room, with its lights.

"What did you do with them?" She demanded.

The sandwich was gone. A bloody, open, fish carcass sat on the plate.

"I told you," he said simply.

Water sloshed over the floor.

Stella shrieked when she saw the flood. It had been coming, but now she was truly seeing it. The building was supposed to be sealed. Airtight. Watertight.

She couldn't understand.

"It's leaking," she said. The water was gaining strength with her acknowledgement of it. "Nellie!" She called. "Doug! Sheila!"

The waters kept rising.

"Come on," said the castaway, and he took her hand.

He tugged her up the stairs, to higher ground. It was smart. It was necessary. But it was hard, all the same. She hadn't found the others. What if they were out there somewhere? Even Anita might be out there somewhere, still, in the thick of this storm.

The Castaway navigated the upper floors with ease, pulling her along. The sea was rising impossibly quickly as it tried to claim them.

She saw where he was going, and she stopped.

"Wait," she said.

"We have to go," he said.

"I need to grab something."

"It won't matter."

"It does."

Stella was a woman in her late forties. She was stubborn. She had been like a mother to the four members of staff who were all, suddenly, gone. Who must, she reasoned, by default, be submerged. She was losing battles left and right and her sanity would be quick to follow if she was no longer the kind of person who would risk it all to go back for something important.

If only she could remember what had been so important.

When she made it to her room, she did not see whatever it was she'd been looking for. In the classy, yet small living quarters, she saw very little sign that she had ever even lived there. There were no personal effects, no fond memories. She could not remember what she had thought to bring.

Her mind was filled, unprompted, with the vision of the dead fish on its fine plate.

Dejectedly, she pulled the comforter from the bed and carried it back to the castaway so that she would not be empty-handed as he led her to the roof.

It was soaked within seconds of making it outside.

The rain was not so heavy, but the waves were now crashing upon the roof of the estate. She wrapped the comforter around herself, and he latched the door.

He took a seat beside where she was bundled up in her freezing blanket.

"I don't understand what's happening," she confessed.

"I wouldn't expect you to."

"It all happened so fast."

"That's because I'm running out of time."

"I *feel* real," she told him, and he gave her the saddest smile.

"I'm sorry."

He wrapped an arm around her, and she let him.

"You never told me your name," she reminded him.

"Have you not figured that out yet?"

But she had.

In a way, she supposed she had known from the second she saw him on the beach. Maybe that was why she had felt so compelled to help him.

The two sat on the roof, and watched in silence as the sea consumed the sky.

L'Arabesque

♥

THE INSTRUCTOR'S VOICE RINGS loud and clear, cutting through the small studio space like a command whistle. "Bras Bas!"

The dancer stands as tall as she can manage, heels together, her toes pointed forward toward the mirror at only a slight diagonal. Her arms rest, rounded, below her belly. Her fingers are dangerously close to touching one another, her hands almost resting against her body. Almost. Even in this preparatory position, she is never allowed to rest.

She is held captive by the anticipation. She has four peers in the room with her, but it feels always as though she is alone with the instructor, who shall pounce on every hesitation.

"First Position."

The dancer's arms rise in front of her. They are still rounded and soft. The ascent must be graceful above all else, for she has now begun in earnest. She is now open to criticism and correction, whether she is ready or not. Her heels press together as the angle of her feet extends. Her left toes point to the left, her right toes to the right, and a perfect, straight line is formed where her weight rests on the floor. She knows she must never be anything less than perfect, and the dread rises with her arms.

She doesn't know if she can do this today.

"Plier," says the instructor.

The dancer folds.

"Relever," says the instructor.

The dancer rises.

"Second Position."

The dancer lets her right foot slide open, still following that invisible horizontal line across the floor. Her right arm mirrors the movement of her leg. Her left leg cannot move at all, but her left arm must subtly adjust to keep the circular effect of her arms.

It should be easy by now, and not something she can risk overthinking. And yet...

She tries to tell herself it won't be so bad.

"Plier."

So she does.

"Relever."

She does that too.

All five of the ballerinas are trapped in a world of their own, and yet they move in unison. Like clockwork.

"Third Position."

Her weight shifts fully to her left leg so she can draw her right foot in, nestling in her right heel into the arch of her left foot, the tip of her right shoe pointed subtly toward the mirror. She knows better than to look at herself for confirmation that the position is right. Her eyes are not allowed to search. They must be as placid and controlled as the rest of her face at all times. Her left arm curls in front of her while her right arm rises to form a crescent above her head. She puts the effort into making even her fingers dainty — as if this will make up for her height or or weight or various other less than perfect features.

She doesn't want to be here.

"Plier," comes the instruction.

There is a pause for her to obey, which she always does.

"Relever."

Again, it is done.

"Fourth position."

Her foot slides forward. For a fleeting moment, she's not sure she can find the spot where it is supposed to stop. This is a thing she has done a thousand times over, but everything feels wrong today. She doesn't trust her muscle memory to guide her as it should. She has only made it this far into the advanced class by never trusting herself entirely.

She is here only by the force of sheer will that pushes her to be something better than she is.

It's exhausting.

She forgets momentarily what to do with her arms. Her left opens up with enough uncertainty as to threaten her balance. She has not felt this clumsy since she was a child. Since she first began.

She has come so far and yet today is as hard as it was the first day. She feels herself sliding back after years and years of effort. She doesn't understand why it's happening. Every class lately has felt worse somehow, but it's never gotten this bad. They haven't even started properly, and she is already on the precipice of failure.

An anger flares inside her that she mustn't show. She is but a sentient desire to purge that weakness from herself once and for all.

Her legs are perfectly straight. Her knees lock to keep them as such, and to hide her nervous wobbling.

Knees are not supposed to lock. Not ever. But the position is held. The silence is held. Her mistakes have not been caught.

"Plier," continues her instructor.

She folds.

"Relever."

She rises.

"Fifth Position."

Her right foot retreats, pressing flat against its partner. Her arms rise above her head, putting the full length of her body on total display. Her feet are parallel lines, touching, her toes pointed in opposite directions. She is supposed to feel elongated here, but for the first time she just feels exposed in this familiar position. She feels sickeningly human, round and lumpy in all the wrong places.

If she were brave enough to look at herself and the other dancers, she knows how many countless ways her body would be found lacking in comparison to theirs.

"Plier."

Her mortal mass of flesh folds.

It feels so unfair.

"Relever."

A sharp pain snags in her guts as she rises.

The dancer makes no sound, and thus, no correction is yet needed.

They begin again, this time on the left.

"First position."

The instructor glares at the dancer, at the twisted look of pain on her face. The dancer is quick to replace the mask that covers such weakness. All the while she curses at herself internally. She forgot to make it all look effortless. She forgot to be graceful, if only in the small lines where her mouth twisted in discomfort. That is enough of a failure. On any other day, it would be enough for a reprimand. The instructor must feel generous for the dancer gets to correct herself without a verbal warning.

"Plier."

Or the instructor feels she is no longer *worth* warning.

That is a disturbing thought.

"Relever."

She rises higher than she knew she could, her feet straining against the weight of her body to lift her up.

"Second position."

It feels good to move the left leg. The knee feels weak from where she foolishly let it lock up before. She can feel the kneecap straining beneath the tights, beneath her skin. To slide into second is to give it some relief, but still, she cannot shake the knowledge that she is too aware of her bones. Not just the kneecap, either. All her bones. They feel heavy and pointed as they move around inside her.

Her toes feel crushed in the little box that traps them. They want to spread out of the delicate point into which they have been molded.

"Plier."

She hides the grimace better this time as she forces her legs to fold.

"Relever."

She struggles to keep it hidden as she rises.

"Third Position."

Usually, the hardest part is getting out of the house. Once she is dressed in her leotard and her tights, and her delicate little wrap skirt, the dread in her chest has loosened enough for her to move with whatever grace she can scrape up for the day.

Most times, she is even able to fake that beautiful dancer's smile.

She can't put her finger on why today feels so drastically different. All she knows is that now there is this pain twisting in her stomach as the instructor speaks.

Still.

She will not throw away all the work for nothing.

"Plier."

She folds.

"Relever."

She rises.

She takes what comfort she can from this excruciating routine.

"Fourth Position."

It is no longer just her stomach and the one knee that hurts. Her arms feel like they may crash under their own weight. The muscles in her neck scream at being held aloft instead of looking down at her cramping body. She can feel her pulse in the pads of her feet as she bends down to the plier. She can feel the blood seeping into the bandages that wrap her battered toes.

There is blood elsewhere, too.

The dancer knows better than to assess the damage, but she can feel the stickiness between her legs. Her brain floods with images of how ridiculous it will look if her pretty pink tights get stained.

She fears disappointing her instructor more than she fears the personal humiliation, but still, there is an urgency in her movements now.

If she can finish the warm-ups, she'll be allowed to sneak away. To figure it out. To do something.

The relever in this position is excruciating. She has never had to use this much force to get her heels off the ground, creasing the hard interior of the shoes.

"Fifth Position."

The routines won't be this bad, she reasons. Dancing makes her feel weightless. It is something she can lose herself in once the music starts, and the constant motion will keep her from feeling any one part of her aching body for too long.

She just has to make it through the warm-ups, she tells herself as she folds.

The positions are all but done, she reckons as she rises.

She just needs to make it to that final arabesque.

"Rond de jambe."

It is too much. The cramping in her gut is too much, and she knows she will never make it through this next couple of minutes.

The dancer asks if she might be excused. Her voice is vague and sounds funny to her own ears. Her toes are clenched. Her whole body is tied up into knots at the thought of what will come. The fever is spreading from her abdomen to the rest of her.

"You are free to go once the warm up has concluded."

She does not explain how warm she already feels. She grits her teeth and imagines that the pain is just more weakness being purged.

Her left foot continues to ache as her right toe stretches forward. She brings it around her body in a perfect half circle. The pain is not so bad yet, but she can see the red stain she leaves through her periphery. Her eyes wander to the floor to confirm that she is not imagining it.

She opens her mouth to ask again and is silenced by a sharp look from the instructor. Surely the instructor has seen the blood, yet her face is furrowed and unsympathetic. The dancer forces her gaze forward once more.

"En l'aire!"

She lifts her leg into the air in front of her to follow the command, and all hell breaks loose within her body.

Her grounded leg throbs when forced to take up her full weight. The knee feels like it may buckle. The blood is seeping down both thighs.

She feels lightheaded. The only thing that keeps her in place standing on one leg is the burning heel that feels like it has melted through her shoe into the ground. Her skin no longer feels feverish, so much as it feels charred.

Something is changing.

Her right leg too is ablaze. Usually her thighs will burn by the end of the exercise, but this is something new. She can feel the muscles pulsing, and tearing, and threatening to turn her flesh inside out if she does not stop.

Her eyes wander to the instructor who is staring at her coldly. It is a silent order to continue the exercise.

There is no mercy in this art.

There is perfection, or there is nothing.

As her leg swings out to the side she can feel the bones in her hips grinding against one another — bones she didn't even know she had that are now cracking and breaking and threatening to pierce her skin with every degree of the ever shifting angle. She can feel that skin puncture and tear as she forces the leg behind her to complete the arc.

She tries not to listen to the *drip, drip, drip* of her blood landing on the floor.

She tries to tell herself she's imagining it.

It cannot possibly look as bad it feels. She does not dare drop her eyes low enough on her reflection to confirm.

There are only nine circles left to complete on this side.

"Rond de jambe," says the instructor again when it is time to switch.

By the time she lowers her right leg, it is more sinew than flesh. The tights are mostly shredded and the small slivers of pink netting that remain are soaked through in blood, plastered to the wet mass of veins underneath.

Her toe is the perfect point of her twisted skeletal structure, and it grinds into the floor with a wet crunch when she tries to stand on it flat.

Her tendrils fill the box of her ballet slipper and prepare themselves to take her weight.

The other girls seem afraid to look.

The dancer doesn't know if they're afraid of her or of the instructor, who has taught them so rigidly that they must not break form.

But the dancer has broken everything about her form, and the unease is thick in the studio.

Her left toe points forward, further forward than it should be able to manage. Her toes on the side are still shaped like toes, but they are grazing the mirror, they are so far away.

"En l'aire!" Calls the instructor.

The dancer's toes stay, abandoned to the floor as her left leg lifts into the air to follow the command again.

The cracking and snapping of her bones elongating has gotten too loud for the other nervous dancers to ignore.

A particularly brave or curious ballerina tears her eyes from where they are supposed to be locked onto themselves in the large mirror. Her head turns slightly, and then not so slightly over to the dancer who is emerging from her cocoon.

Snap! Crunch! Crack!

She screams.

The sound is one that our dancer might have made had she been the first one to see the change in herself.

She had been lost in her thoughts, in the deep black pools of her own eyes, just as she had been taught.

When she hears her own sound coming from another's mouth, she snaps in an entirely new way.

She snaps internally.

She breaks free from the thrall of the instructor.

She claims her new existence as her body has already done.

The dancer begins to dance.

She was not always a dancer. She had been a little girl once, who had only dreamed of the stage. She had loved the ballerinas with their long legs and their sparkly outfits. She had loved them for their beauty.

She had begged her mother for the lessons and had been denied.

The little girl would not give up.

Her mother told her over and over that she was soft. That she was spoiled. That she did not have what it took to become a dancer. That she would never in all her days look so perfect.

It was all she had ever wanted.

So she kept asking. When her mother finally relented, she had gone to all the classes she could. Even when they were terrible. Even when she couldn't do the steps.

She'd be so relieved when an hour at the studio ended, and she could go home. Even as she got better and the steps got easier, she never stopped trying to be perfect. The sense of dread never entirely went away.

She has been beating it back for so long, that feeling of dread that came with practice. The feeling of inadequacy when she struggled. The deep revulsion she felt with her own short, stunted body that was so far from perfect.

So why has she stayed?

It is for the moments like this. The moments in between the corrections and the glares and the pain, when she is weightless. When she is dancing.

She has never been so bold before.

She has never heard the music in her head so loudly that she feels the need to take off before the warm up has even concluded.

There is a certain freedom that has come with her transformation. Her body has finally responded to the pleas of her heart.

It has broken through the barrier of pain that had previously been so limiting. Her mind is now one with her form and it is absolutely flying across the studio.

She begins with the girl who screamed.

It isn't even anger, past that initial flash of righteous injustice. It's just natural. It's what the music calls for. She glides over, spinning, barely taking in the room as she makes it to the girl. Her long limbs wrap around her victim then release quickly, so that the scared witness crunches and cracks in the same way as our dancer.

This girl is the one who was weak.

She was the one who could not survive the transformation into perfection, whereas the true dancer is already through the worst of it.

The screams rise in the throats of the other girls, singing the chorus that she feels in her core. Their blood wishes to join her, and she is quick to comply.

She spins and leaps through them, faster than could be imagined, too liquid for them to hold on to and far too strong to push past. Her little feet bound and twirl and keep her at both exits at once. Her arms are long and twisted and move like they are caught in the glorious scarlet whirlwind that her new form emulates.

Her fingers, such as they were, point and harden, and slick the exposed bone where the flesh has fallen away. They are like knives unto themselves and they are quick to peel the other dancers into the most delicate spirals of skin. Red blood splashes across the wall and floor and ceiling in a pattern too beautiful for any artist.

No amount of mortal choreography could do justice to this display of death. They are a company. They are one flesh. One dance. One final song that has reached its crescendo.

The dying notes are still ringing in the dancer's ears before she sees the instructor.

The tall woman looks as harsh as ever. One lone soldier dressed in black amongst a sea of tattered pink and red. Her hair is pulled back into a perfect, salt and pepper bun. Her pale cheek is spattered with the remnants of her pupils.

The dancer steps forward.

She expects fear. She expects the instructor to back away. To order her to stop.

It is a different kind of command that falls from the woman's mouth.

"L'arabesque."

The dancer pauses.

Words are a clumsy means of communication in comparison to the music. The sound is too blunt and mortal. It is amazing how far she has come from that life in just a matter of a few minutes once she made the decision to truly break away.

The instructor is patient. She tries again. "L'arabesque." There is just the hint of a smile on her lips.

The dancer's body recalls before the words can take any sort of shape in her brain. It is a pose that her form is eager to recreate in its own, stunning glory. It will be the beginning of her true freedom and the end of all else she has known.

Joint after joint after joint of the long limb that was formally a leg extends behind her, arcing up toward the ceiling as she balances on the exposed bones of her left foot. The needle point of her conjoined toes drills down into the floor as it takes her weight.

Her left arm stretches out to the side in an elegant coil to help aid balance. Her torso tilts forward over curve of what were once hip bones. Her back arches in the most inhuman angles.

She lifts her right arm up from where it dangles at her side and pierces it quickly through the soft belly of her instructor. She lifts up, cutting up through skin and meat and organs until her limb lodges in a rib and the instructor's feet rise off the floor.

The dancer's arm takes its proper place in the pose, above her head, and her instructor is looking down at her. The guts are hanging out of the large gash that cuts the woman almost completely in half, and her blood and excrement tumble to the floor.

The dancer has never seen her look so messy before. Nor so happy.

As the light leaves the instructor's eyes, the last thing she sees is her creation. It took hours and hours of work to get her here, but the dancer is at last, perfect.

She tries to whisper this sentiment in guttural, burbling French, but it is too late.

Content, the dancer holds her final pose.

Enlightenment

♥

Twenty-four other people had made the descent down to Challenger Deep before her. Twenty-four pioneers of science had seen the lowest point in the ocean — a deep depression of the Mariana Trench. Twenty-four elated mortals had made the return trip to the surface with a new outlook on life. In this regard, Ana would not be the twenty-fifth.

She came to, hoping it had all just been a terrible nightmare. The Event certainly didn't represent reality, as her scientific mind had learned to process it. Her surroundings gave her little reason to suspect that it had been a figment of her imagination, however.

"Hello?" She asked, feeling her voice crack. "Hello? Carter? Carter, come in!"

She straightened her posture as she looked over the control panel of her small submersible vessel. Immediately, she regretted what she saw. The navigation screen was cracked in one corner and there was no sign of light or life in her coms.

I'm dead, she thought. *I'm fucking dead.*

Suddenly, the life-changing horror she had borne witness to earlier didn't seem as important as the smaller, life-threatening dread she was now facing. In her panic, the vehicle seemed to be crushing her. What had felt like a cozy, protective bubble on the way down was making the weight of its reinforced steel known.

She fumbled with what now seemed an obscene amount of safety restraints, keeping her confined to the chair. She had no plans as to where she'd go when she was freed. There was nowhere she *could* go. She didn't even have enough room to stand properly in her craft, but that didn't stop her trying.

She didn't even make it far enough for her head to hit the domed ceiling before she fell, and found herself wedged in the small strip of floor between her chair and the wall. The air felt thin and stale. Her sense of balance was off kilter — as was the rest of her damn world.

She pulled herself into a sitting position and tried to regulate both her breathing and her pulse.

Have I lost life support? How long was I out? How much air do I have left?

She shook off the questions. They were important and would need answered, but she'd need to calm down and take them one at a time. After another breath, the air didn't feel as stale as she'd feared, and her critical thinking began to return.

Standing was a challenge. Aside from the pins and needles in her legs, Ana's head felt too heavy for her body. She felt, more than saw, that the submersible was no longer upright.

A bad sign.

The cables that had lowered her down were specifically designed not to let her twist too far. This angle wouldn't have been within the threshold, which could only mean that her support cables had been damaged in the quake.

Or something happened to the ship.

Ana fought off the very distinct image of what that 'thing' might have been. She sat back in her chair and looked over her limited resources for information. All that was left to do was to take stock of her situation so she could plan accordingly.

She flipped the switch for the com on and off a few times, listening attentively for the sound of a crackling speaker, or any attempted communication from her crew. "Hello? Hello?" She tried.

Nothing.

What was worse than the silence from the speaker was the knowledge that she couldn't hear her own voice, either.

Ana raised her hands to her ears and felt panic surge again when they came back red and sticky.

The sound must have ruptured my eardrums, she thought. Then, with terror, *that means the sound was real.*

If the Event had not been a nightmare, then the last thing she could afford to do was panic. She tried to switch on the auxiliary lighting for the control panel so she could have visual confirmation as to whether or not the coms were working.

No auxiliary lights came on.

Ana had lost all communication with the U.S.S. Carter, positioned nearly 11,000 meters above her. It had been her lifeline and her ticket back to the surface. That thing must have shaken loose her submersible craft. Enlightenment, as she had called it, was now sunk.

Still, there was some cause for hope.

Losing the coms was bad, but it was not detrimental on its own. Working it through calmly, Ana had to conclude that some of the lines between her and the ship must still be connected. Enlightenment had not sustained serious damage. If she'd been cast aside too far, or if the vessel had been harmed, she would have already been crushed by the seven atmospheres worth of pressure surrounding her.

But I'm not crushed. I'm still breathing. I'm not frozen. I can still see.

That was her next mystery. With the lights off inside the craft, she shouldn't have been able to see a thing. While she was grateful, that was not the case, it was important to find where the light was coming from so she knew what was still working. She looked around once more to pinpoint the source, just realize it had literally been in front of her the entire time.

The display.

Due to the solid gray mass it depicted, Ana had mistakenly thought her display screen had gone out with everything else. But it wasn't blacked out or broken, and was lighting up the inside of her craft with a dim, sanity-saving glow.

Ana's heart soared.

The display screen was still intact. More importantly, it was still feeding back information from her cameras. It meant that not only had she captured the Event, but that the outside of her vehicle was still operational.

It means I'm still getting power from above.

Enlightenment, ironically perhaps, would have gone dark on its own. The emergency power would go to pumping in her small amount of oxygen reserves and regulating temperature. It wasn't hooked up to the cameras or lights that were mounted outside the craft.

Whatever happened didn't entirely sever me from Carter.

There had been other signs, like the fact she was still alive, but actually seeing this with her own eyes gave her something to latch onto.

The spark of hope was enough to kick her brain back into action.

The gray screen before her was likely a result of the light being reflected back by the sediment, which she had seen for herself get disrupted merely five minutes after landing. The visual effect would be like high beams in the fog, making visibility worse until all the silt and sand settled back into place. In the ocean, she knew that would take a while. But it gave her something to wait for, and a way to measure time.

That's all I need.

It was possible that she hadn't been out all that long. If she'd lost the coms before she had issued her warning to the crew, there was still a chance they *could* pull her up, but just hadn't started yet. They had strict orders to retract the lines only by command, or if the coms were down for more than an hour. They had talked about that particular protocol many, many times. Ana had wanted the cutoff point to be longer, and never in her life had she been so grateful for the caution of her team. Even if they weren't pulling her up now, they'd have acknowledged the lack of communication, and would be watching their clocks.

Sixty minutes and she would be on her way up with video evidence of what she'd seen. She could go over it again and again until there was a reasonable explanation for it all.

I just need to wait it out.

Ana sat back in her captain's chair for the undertaking, though she had never felt less like a captain in her entire life. She had gotten as far as she had in her career by her practical approaches to things, and no small amount of tenacity. She was, in a single word, proactive. Even though she knew what she must do, the passivity of it bothered her. Sitting, waiting, letting her future hang in someone else's hands; these were the things that she hated most about the concept of these expeditions. They were cons of the mission, yes, but until recently they had been so in an abstract way. She had never expected to be facing them head on so directly.

It's only sixty minutes.

Within just five minutes, she found herself fiddling with the control panel. If she'd be forced to wait, she wouldn't do it idly.

"They'll pull me up," she repeated to herself as she checked the buttons one by one for any sign of power. She had never realized how much comfort her own voice could bring her in moments of isolation — not until she could no longer hear it. She continued talking all the same, like a prayer in the only thing she could find to believe in. Her crew. "They'll pull me up. At the end of an hour, they'll pull me up."

Unless they're dead.

The longer the silence pressed upon her and Enlightenment stood still, the more certain she became that the hour must have already passed. Then it became harder for her to block out the negative thoughts. Eventually, it was impossible to forget about what she had seen, and what a creature of that magnitude could have done to the ship.

A vision played out in her mind of her crew being torn limb from limb by the inky shape she'd only glimpsed.

But it was too big to tear them limb from limb, she thought grimly. *It would have just crushed them.*

She tried not to think about that, or the creature, if that's what it had been. She had to try to hold out hope that it had been something else. Some sort of....what? Oil deposit? The world's largest mass of sentient seaweed? Origin of Vantablack?

The thing, whatever it was, seemed utterly unclassifiable. Like many of the other creatures at this level, it moved more like a liquid than a solid. Yet it had been massive in a way she could barely comprehend, and she was sure she'd only seen a part of it. Even from that glimpse, it made no sense that its body composition was of water, because she hadn't been able to see through it. Only that shouldn't have been possible.

A creature with a body mass like that should have been crushed under the pressure this far down. It's why the only things surviving at that level of the ocean were snail fish and sea cucumbers.

She wanted to be comforted by these bits of rational thinking and trick herself into believing that it wasn't a creature at all. It would make more sense for it to be anything but alive. It had moved upward with such purpose. That was anecdotal, projecting, and unscientific, but Ana felt deep down that it was true.

The implications were simply mind-boggling.

Maybe my mind was *boggled.*

She thought of the crash, being knocked unconscious — possibly concussed. She wondered if there was a chance of brain damage, hallucinations from a lobe that had been hit the wrong way. Then she thought to her split ear drums, and wondered what had made the sound, if not for that creature.

That horrid sound will be the last thing I hear.

It was the sound of nightmares. Of worlds created and dying and screaming for retribution all in one terrible breath. No godly creature could have made that shriek.

Even if Ana had been the type to idle before, she would have craved something to take her mind off of her slipping sanity as she recalled the monstrous thing. With 'waiting' being the entirety of her survival plan, that anomaly was the only logical thing to consider.

One final mystery to ponder before I die.

If wondering was bad, then the confirmation was a million times worse.

She was fiddling with the buttons, now two or three at a time, as if hitting the right combination of them could do the impossible, when her attention fell to the display screen again. The image was not coming in clearly, but it was hard to ignore what she saw.

Enlightenment sat, teetering over the edge of a great chasm.

It confirmed then, what she had seen, and what she had tried so hard not to believe. For as long as she had studied the ocean, Challenger Deep had been the deepest point. Until Ana had seen it crack open for the creature to emerge.

I was here to witness the beginning of the end.

Ana screamed. She slammed her fist down on her chair, a redirection from the screen; which was where she truly wanted to strike.

She was done fiddling. She was done waiting. She was, above all, done questioning her sanity down in her steel tomb. Since there was nothing else for her to do, she screamed.

Profanities like she had never uttered fell from her lips and tasted better than she could have hoped. Oxygen and dry throat and busted eardrums be damned. There was a rage in her that she'd never known at the incomprehensible nature of it all. She hoped she could bring that monster back, just so she could look it in the eyes and tell her she didn't give a damn if it killed her.

She had made it further than anyone believed she could. She'd been told all her life that she dreamed too big and wanted too much and she had proven them all wrong with this mission. She had been there to witness the emergence of the biggest disruption the world would ever know, and what had it gotten her? Her discovery, along with her footage and her story would all belong to the next person to make the trip. If anyone dared brave the ocean after this, that is. Maybe she would be the last, and who knew if she'd even be remembered for it. The unfairness of it all made her want to burst.

It wasn't until her throat was raw and her chest burned that she allowed her outburst to end. When the anger was out, she felt hollow, like there had been nothing else inside her body. The display image of the chasm seemed to stare at her, but she had nothing to hide from it.

It had already taken everything from her. She curled her legs up to her chest, tucked her head into them, and cried herself back to a state of calm acceptance.

She couldn't remember the last time she'd cried at all, but she couldn't think of a better place or time to truly let go. She was grateful to find an ounce of tranquility on the other side of the breakdown.

Maybe they had it worse up top.

The creature was swimming up at an alarming speed when Ana had seen it. If her crew hadn't heard the warning she'd shouted at them to leave, they'd have had no idea what was coming their way. They might not have believed her, even if they had heard. There was a non-zero chance that Ana would outlive them, if the monster had continued its trajectory at that rate. If her gut was right, there was a non-zero chance she already had outlived them.

But I'm ready to go.

Maybe it had been an hour since the Event. Maybe longer. Maybe it had been an eternity. Staring into the incomprehensible had, for the first time, made her accept.

Her death, like her existence, meant very little down on the ocean floor. She was nothing but a blip, soon to be snuffed out. If her lifelines did get severed, it would be suffocation or freezing. Dehydration would probably get her first else wise. None of her suffering would be so bad, in the grand scheme of things perhaps, but it was still an intimate tragedy for her, as an individual.

Plus, there was the temptation. She was a dead woman anyway, and she was on the very edge of going deeper into the earth than any human had ever gone.

"It's a shame I couldn't see the rest of it."

As if answering a prayer, she felt turbulence in the water around her. The thing was the abyss made flesh, and it had returned to grant her one final wish.

Support lines to Enlightenment were severed.

The vehicle began to rock forward.

Ana buckled in with curiosity, about to see what no human had ever, or should ever see.

Imaginary, But Very Real

♥

"Mom?"

"Just a minute, Brady."

"Mom."

Mommy looked down at Brady with an impatient, serious look. It was the sort of look that said he'd better have something dang important he wanted to talk about. It needed to be worth interrupting her conversation with her new, nice, blonde mommy-friend.

Brady wasn't concerned about that.

This was important.

"Jesse is missing."

Mommy rolled her eyes. Apparently, she didn't think this was so important after all — though he couldn't imagine why. Jesse was his best friend.

Brady looked around the park again, just to confirm that he was really gone. He'd only looked away for one second. A single second, and suddenly his best friend in the whole world was gone. Missing.

"Missing," he said again, louder and slower, just in case she had misunderstood the first time. It was the middle of the day at a public park. It wasn't super busy, but there were still a couple parents and bored-looking babysitters sitting around. There were people. It would have to be a scary person to take Jesse in broad daylight where they might have been seen.

"I'm sure he's just hiding, dear."

The blonde mommy-friend looked around, concerned. Her eyes fell on a little girl in a blue dress and bright pink sunglasses. She had blonde pigtails. It was probably the woman's daughter.

See? Brady wanted to ask his mother. *See? She wants to make sure that everything's okay.*

"Who is Jesse?" She asked.

"No one," Mommy said, trying to brush it off. She had another special mommy-look on her face, one that said it was nothing and that she'd explain it later. Later, when Brady wasn't around. Only he had no intention of letting her ignore the problem, not when he had an opportunity to get help for his friend. He was not about to let her say that Jesse was no one.

"He's my best friend!"

Mommy-friend looked alarmed, which was exactly how Brady felt. He was glad to see that expression on the face of an adult. That was the look mommy should have, instead of one of her special ones.

"*Imaginary* friend," his mom explained.

Brady hated when she did that, when she explained for him. When she ignored his problems, and Jesse. He especially hated it when she used that word.

Imaginary.

He could feel the tears hot in his eyes, from anger as well as from fear. He was six, and he knew he was too old to cry. He didn't, but it was pretty close. He yelled, instead.

"You said that imaginary doesn't mean not real!" He shouted. "You said that!"

Mommy looked surprised.

Brady was a little surprised, too.

He had never done that before, yelled at Mommy like that. He didn't want to, only she wasn't understanding what was happening. She looked apologetic to her new friend, the way she looked apologetic to daddy sometimes. She never looked like that at Brady, because Mommies were never supposed to be wrong when it came to their children.

"I did say that, Brady—"

"Then, if he's real, we have to help him!"

He usually didn't interrupt her, either.

The salt was really starting to sting his eyes, though. He could not contain it much longer.

"I'm sorry about this," his mommy said to her friend, who gave a small smile that was too sweet. Too understanding. This too was a special mommy look that Brady recognized, even though it was on the face of a stranger.

"Mom!" He shouted again.

"Brady," she said. Her eyes were angry. He'd be in trouble later, he knew, but it would be worth it if they found Jesse. "What was Jesse doing when he first went missing?"

He didn't like the way she said Jesse's name. It was slower, and with a higher voice. She said his name like he wasn't real.

"We were playing."

"Playing what?"

"We were about to start hide and seek."

"Was it his turn to hide?"

He was ashamed then, but not because he thought she was right. He could see that Mommy and mommy-friend were still smiling down at him. He wished he was taller, and that they would take him seriously.

"He was going to hide first. But we hadn't started yet," he explained.

"Are you sure?"

"Yes!"

"Maybe he's just a really good hider."

"Mom, we hadn't started yet!"

He hoped she wouldn't see the tear that was starting down his cheek, but she must have. Before he knew it, she was kneeling down and her hands were on his shoulders.

Yes. This was the mommy he liked. This was how she was when she was taking him seriously, when she was listening.

"Brady," she said.

This was it. She was going to help.

"Yes?"

"I want you to take a deep breath."

He hated when she told him to do that, which is what she always did. He did it anyway, and it helped, which it always did.

"Jesse likes to play games with you sometimes, right?"

"Right," he mumbled.

"Isn't it possible that he hid while you weren't looking? To mess with you? As a game?"

That wasn't what *missing* meant.

She didn't understand, possibly because Jesse was not her imaginary but very real friend.

Part of Brady wanted very much to believe that she was right. If mommy was right, then Jesse wasn't for real missing, and nothing would be wrong. Brady would feel a little silly, because he would have been panicked over nothing, but that happened sometimes. Wasn't that better than having something to panic about?

"Maybe," he admitted. He didn't believe it, but he wanted to.

"Then I'll make you a deal, okay, buddy?"

"What kind of deal?"

"You go look for Jesse. Look *really* good, okay? Look everywhere, and if you really can't find him, I'll come help."

Part of his brain relaxed, just to know that mommy would be there when he needed her. She was taking his fear seriously, if not him. The other part of his brain wondered if it wouldn't be too late by the time he finished looking. He was worried it was too late now.

It would only take more time to fight, though. Plus, maybe, just maybe, she was right.

"You promise?"

"I promise," she swore.

So that was it. Set in stone. Mommy got angry sometimes, but she kept her promises. That was what mattered.

"Okay," he said, and he turned back to the playground.

"But you have to look really good, okay?" She added.

"Okay."

"Promise?" She called after him.

He could not help but smile, if only a little bit. "I promise."

The smile didn't last long. There were so many places to look, and all the equipment felt larger than it had when he had been standing atop it with Jesse.

He started by looking underneath, first. Crying had made his face warm, as had the yelling and the running to Mommy and running back. Searching in the shade underneath, the playground was gloomy, and spookier than he would have believed earlier, but it gave him a break from the hot sun. Still, he didn't linger too long. Around every corner, he expected to see an evil man in a trench coat, or a monster rising out of the mulch, ready to take him to Jesse.

He climbed the plastic rock wall up to the railing. He ran across both bridges. He peered down the kiddie slides. He climbed up onto the plastic to make sure Jesse wasn't sitting on top of them. He looked behind the walls with the rotating blocks. He looked at the big ship wheel before going down the big, twisting slide all alone.

He had never done that before.

It was almost fun until he got to the bottom and turned around, and realized that Jesse wasn't going to come out behind him.

He started crying then, really crying, like he hadn't done for a long time.

There weren't any other kids around to see, thankfully, but he was loud enough that mommy came running over.

"Brady?"

"I can't find him, mom! He's not here, Jesse's gone!"

She hugged him close and then pushed him back a bit, with her hands on his shoulders like he liked. "Brady, I want you to listen to me, okay?"

He was crying too hard to answer, so he just nodded.

"I want you to close your eyes, alright?"

He closed his eyes.

This was the part where she'd tell him to take a deep breath and he wouldn't want to, but he would, and it would make him feel better.

Only she didn't say that.

He couldn't feel her hands on his shoulders anymore.

He didn't open his eyes for a long time after that. He knew when he did, that mommy would be missing too.

Just like Jesse.

You'll Just Be Nothing

♥

Joanne's fingers were always sore after a show, but she pressed them into the fretboard anyway. She missed the days when all her problems could simply be bled away by her clumsy hand.

"Jo, you decent?"

"I've never been fuckin' decent."

Her answer went ignored as Jerry was already swinging the door open to the shitty little closet space they had been told was the VIP room.

At the height of Obstantine's fame, they would have been offended at what the venue had offered them here in way or rec space. These days, nothing much mattered. They had lost their diva a long time ago, and with Jo fronting the group, the others fell in line. They kept mostly to the tour bus, and she was just grateful that they were still considered headline material somewhere.

"What do you want, Jerry?"

"You ready to see the kid?"

"What kid? I don't want to see a—"

Jo cut herself off when she saw the youthful face poking around the doorframe.

The rather androgynous stranger at least looked to be the high school/college variety of kid, and not a literal child. Jo was already a fourth of the way into her post-show bottle, and would not have had an easy time keeping her language clean in front of a minor. Whatever filter she might once have had was now a distant memory, killed by years of drinking, drugs, and a hard life on the road.

"Hi," said the kid nervously.

"Hey," she answered.

"Jo, this is Kai. You agreed to do the meet and greet, remember?"

Jerry knew as well as she did that she could barely remember this morning, let alone anything before that. It was as polite a segue as she was like to get, however, and the kid was already there.

"Right, of course. Sit."

"You two gonna be alright in here?"

"Sure, fine. Oh, wait." She looked over to her unexpected guest, trying to determine if they were old enough for alcohol. Their face was round, but with defined cheeks and a firm jaw, making it impossible to guess an age. She decided she probably shouldn't be drinking with a young fan anyway. She'd never do anything, but she was aware of the optics.

They were both staring at her.

Shit.

"Sorry. Just, uh, do you want a coke or something?"

"No," Kai answered. "Thanks though, but I'm alright."

Jerry met her eyes, silently asking if he could leave. Jo nodded. Whatever it was she had agreed to, she was as ready as she was going to get for it.

"So, do you want an autograph or something?"

Lame.

Pathetic.

Even the visitor — Kai, apparently, — didn't look interested in that. *Never meet your heroes, kid.*

"No, thanks. It's not that."

Jo wished she could remember under what circumstances she had agreed to this, which could save her the embarrassment of guessing.

"Private show?" She asked, looking down hopefully to the Strat in her hands. If it were up to her, she never would have quit playing in the first place. She would be up on that stage until the crowd left of their own accord, and she'd still be going long after they left. "I take requests."

Kai fidgeted around some, looking almost as uncomfortable as Jo felt. "I was actually hoping we could talk?"

Jo cringed involuntarily at the request. She had never been good with words that weren't scripted, and she didn't like the familiar nature of the request. Like she was the kid's mom, or fucking guidance counselor or some shit. But what could she say?

"Uh, sure."

She set the guitar down on the couch beside her. She poured herself a glass of whiskey that she had been drinking straight from the bottle prior, just so she had something to do with her hands.

"First, I want to thank you. You know, for the music. The show was really good tonight."

"Oh. Uh, yeah. No problem."

She'd never been thanked for her music before. In fan letters and stuff, maybe, back when she'd still read them. But never in person like that.

"I've been listening to your guys' stuff for so long — since I was little."

It was always a weird feeling to meet someone that grew up on their music. It was also funny to hear the youth in front of her refer to their littleness like it was a long time ago, and not just a handful of tours past.

Time was really one of those things that could fuck you.

"That's cool."

Jo wasn't trying to be dismissive, but she was distracted. Her fingers were itching to play, and she didn't have anything to add to this conversation.

"I've been listening to a lot more of it recently. Going back to some of the old stuff. It kept me really good company in the hospital."

It clicked in.

"Oh, shit." Jo remembered it all at once. "You're the kid from that video."

Kai grimaced. "That's me."

"Sorry. Uh..."

"No. It's alright. It's what people know me for. I'm sure it's probably why you agreed to meet me?"

Fuck.

He wasn't far off the mark. Jo could remember the conversation now, albeit vaguely. She'd been moved by the interview clip, which had gone viral several months back.

The Cursed Kai Perkins.

Sort of an odd duck, Jo remembered thinking when watching the interview, but that was alright. In the punk scene, that was always alright, and the kid had clearly seen some shit.

The clip had started out like one of those heart-warming, Christian fluff pieces, an interview shining light on the good work of the children's hospital. It had taken a dark turn very quickly.

Kai, *Miss Perkins*, as the reporter had insisted on calling him, had been in and out of the center fourteen times over the last ten years, and been declared legally dead twice.

Jo had gotten it in her head after watching the footage that she'd wanted to write a song about him.

Brush with death, or flirting with death, or some such nonsense.

So it had felt like fate when Jerry said that the boy had actually reached out to them about trying to book a VIP pass to their Columbus show. He'd had a whole spiel ready about the good PR the band needing good PR, and he must have been surprised when she'd readily agreed.

Fortunately for her, she hadn't had to explain why.

Nothing had ever come of the song idea past a little riff she'd played with for a week or so. In fact, she had nearly forgotten all about it. It had been years since she'd written any new material that wasn't pulled straight from one of her old notebooks and just spruced up a little. Whatever inspiration the kid had given her, it had been fleeting.

Now she felt like even more of an ass for forgetting about it, and not recognizing him, and not having a song or anything real to say. She felt guilty also for the long silence that was stretching on for too long between them.

"So, uh. What can I do for you? What do you want to talk about?"

"I was actually hoping we could talk about you."

She laughed and took an ill-advised sip of Jack. "The music is a lot more interesting than me."

Kai shook his head. "No, I don't think that's true. You did an interview back in 2009 with Arsenal Mag that resonated with me."

Jo felt more awful and drank more deeply before fessing up. "I don't know if I remember that one."

"They asked you about why you picked up the guitar?"

Jo nodded, like the question had been special, like she hadn't been asked that same thing a million goddamned times. "Oh, yeah. Sure."

"You said you thought the guitar looked the coolest."

She had actually done it to impress the lead guitarist of her favorite band back at the time, but there was no quicker way to lose her cred than to admit such a thing. "Yeah, I remember that."

"You said that once you started playing, you appreciated the sound of the instrument more."

It was interesting, hearing her own experiences parroted back at her. It was almost like having a conversation with her younger self. The corners of her mouth lifted some. "Yeah, I did."

Kai lit up at that, taking the half-smile as encouragement. His voice got faster, more animated. "And there was this thing you said, that you started hearing guitars louder than other instruments after that. You could pick those lines of music out from the ensemble, because they were so familiar?"

"Like a friend," she said. She couldn't remember the interview, but she could remember that sense of wonder when she had started learning.

"Yes!" Kai beamed at her, and she smiled back. "You said it was like hearing the voice of an old friend."

"That really stuck with you, huh?"

"It did. I have something like that, that's happening to me." His expression suddenly fell, growing serious. "I never knew how to describe it until I read that interview."

Jo shifted on the couch. "Do you play?"

"No. Not exactly."

She had to wait a minute for the explanation. She sipped at her drink and waited for the silence to become unbearable. Just when she was about to crack, Kai spoke again.

"I've never told anyone this before."

"Okay."

"And I don't expect you to believe me. But I just need to tell someone."

Jo shrugged. Admitting her skepticism didn't seem like a good way to move the conversation forward, so she just said, "try me."

Kai leaned forward and looked at her, gauging her reaction. "I can hear when people are about to die."

Jo sipped at her whiskey.

It was the only thing she could think of to do that didn't give away her incredulity. How the hell was she supposed to respond to a thing like that?

"I know how it sounds," Kai said. "But that's the thing. I've just spent enough time around death that I can pick it up through the other noise. Like it's a friend, whispering to me. I didn't know what was happening until I read that interview, and then something clicked."

Jo wished Jerry hadn't left the room. He probably wouldn't save her life if Kai turned out to be one of those crazy, knife-wielding fans she'd heard horror stories about, but he could at least be a deterrent as a witness. She decided her best course was to just play along.

"I mean, there has to be a perk to that, right? If you hear death coming, he can't sneak up on you."

Jo had only meant it as "no more hospital trips," but Kai took it a different way in his eagerness. "Yes! Exactly! That's how I've been managing to do it! It's how I've stayed alive."

"Right. Well, that's good. That's, uh, really good."

"Only, I hear it *all* the time. I thought it would get better when I wasn't a patient anymore but it's even worse in the city, being around all those people. I can't be out on the streets, I can't drive, I can't go shopping without maybe hearing that someone is about to pass. And now that I'm living with my dad again, it's gotten a lot worse."

"Is your dad sick?" She asked, forgetting that the whole thing was some kind of delusion.

"My dad is trying to kill me."

"Oh."

She was in dangerous territory. She wondered if there was a number she could call. The police weren't likely to be helpful in a mental health crisis, and she didn't want to pick up the reputation of narc, but she couldn't let this kid confess all these things to her and then walk away.

"All those accidents, you know, those near misses that I've had? They weren't accidents at all. He's just really good at making them look that way. And now that everyone already believes I'm cursed..."

"It's going to get a lot less suspicious as the accidents keep happening?"

She didn't buy into any of it, but she understood why he'd be concerned if he believed all he'd said so far.

"Exactly."

For a minute, she decided to entertain the idea.

"So why does your dad want to kill you?"

"He always wanted a son." Kai paused. "But he didn't want a son like me."

An odd duck, she had called him when she had seen the interview.

But she knew it was more than that. Even if she didn't understand all the nuances of identity the way this new generation broke them down, she remembered what it was like to be an outcast and a disappointment.

"Right."

"I'm scared," Kai admitted softly.

KILL YOUR DARLINGS

Something in her heart broke for the kid. She remembered that feeling, too. Not with her parents, who had kicked her out young, but what had passed for a home life after that. She remembered dying to say those same two words to someone, but knowing that her bus and band and very livelihood was on the line if she came clean.

What she didn't know was what she could do now, or why he was opening up to her. She'd never gotten that help. She couldn't even imagine what it might look like to offer it to someone else now.

"I'm sorry," she said.

"I was hoping maybe you could help me."

She winced. "Listen, kid. Do you have a friend you could stay with? I'm on the road another couple months, and I can't exactly take a young fan across state lines, you know?"

"I don't want to live with you."

Relief flooded Jo. Then concern. "What do you want?"

"I want you to show me how to kill him."

Down went the rest of Jo's whiskey. She let it burn her throat and sit in her stomach for a minute. Not that it helped.

"I'm going to pretend I didn't hear that."

"It will be self defense."

"It's not self-defense if it's premeditated."

"But—"

"And even if I wanted to help you with this, and didn't mind it making me an accessory, I don't know why you think I would know what to do."

"Because I've heard You'll Just Be Nothing."

Jo's heart stopped.

The room spun.

She had said so. She had told the others she didn't want that song to ever see the light of day.

"It's a B-Side," they had told her.

"He would want us to play it."

"We have to put it on there for him."

"Miss Taylor?"

She tried to focus on the boy's face. She said something she hadn't said in over fifteen years. "I think I've had too much to drink."

"I'm not trying to accuse you of anything. I think I understand why you did it."

She looked him in the eyes, her tone as deadpan as she could make it. "I don't know what you're talking about."

"You'll Just Be Nothing," he said calmly. "Track seven off Get A Life."

She knew the album. She knew the fucking song.

"And?"

"I know what happened on that track. I know you killed Harrison Lee."

When was the last time she'd heard that name?

"Harrison," she forced her voice to remain steady, but her hands were shaking readily as she went to pour herself another drink, "OD'd."

"But you were there, weren't you?"

She could still see him lying on the floor, foaming at the mouth whenever she closed her eyes.

"Of course not. He had the studio to himself that day."

"But you finished his track."

"I don't know what you're talking about."

But she did.

It wasn't possible. She had checked the tape over a hundred times to make sure that his gargles couldn't be heard. That he was safely outside her sound-proofed recording area when she had finished that final bridge and shut off the equipment.

Kai didn't look like he was intentionally trying to torment her, or blackmail her, as she had feared would happen for so many years if anyone were to find out. He didn't look like a murderer when he spoke, either.

"I'm not accusing you of anything. I know that he hurt you."

Rumors.

She couldn't hide the rumors. She could just make sure he died in the studio he booked alone, and that she had an alibi for when he would have finished.

"I'm sorry about your dad," she said.

Jo didn't know what to think about Cursed Kai Perkins, or his affinity for death, or his murderous father. But she believed he was in trouble, and that he was the only person who had ever tried to absolve her of the worst thing she had ever done.

"You're not going to help me, are you?"

"I hope you get... whatever help you need. Really, I do."

He smiled at her so sadly. "Can I ask one more thing?"

She nodded, her mouth dry.

"Would you play a song for me before I go?"

She was eager to pick up the guitar, to carve some sanity out of the silence. "What song?"

Kai looked at her expectantly, and her hands trembled again.

"I haven't played it since that night."

"Please? I've never heard the whole thing without that sound in the back."

He sounded so sad, and sincere, that for a minute she almost believed he could hear something in it that no one else could.

"I don't know if I remember it."

"Would you try?"

Her fingers felt stiff as she fought to recall, but the muscle memory served well enough after the first couple bars. She remembered how scared she had been all those early years. She remembered having nowhere to go. She remembered how he threatened her, even as her dry voice sang out the words he'd written.

> "And what will you be?
> Baby, what will you be?
> You'll just be nothing
> When you don't have me."

The years of drugs and alcohol and touring had tried to blot him away, but his shadow had always been just behind her.

How many years would Kai get, if she didn't step up and help him?

Her voice was shaking by the final chorus, a brief pause filling the air. It was where the drum solo would have gone if she weren't playing alone.

In the silence, she could hear something missing, not just the drums, not just the audio mixing. There was supposed to be the sound of closure with this track. There was a healing, cathartic sound of a bad person who would never again use his instrument to spread sweet lies. She could not hear it exactly, but she could feel its absence.

She let her last chord die in the air, and she didn't start the final bridge.

There was something bigger she could do, to really help the kid.

Until He Starves

♥

She is beautiful, so long as he does not look her in the eyes. He keeps his gaze instead focused on the roiling waves, their attempts to devour the shore below. It would be a long drop, the thought of which should scare him. It doesn't. He is more afraid of her stare. He cannot see it, but can feel how it penetrates through his flesh and to his very soul instead.

All the while, her sisters whisper all around him.

"Do it."

"Jump."

"Make it end."

"Only you can stop this."

"Do it now."

"Tell me," she says. "What is it that they say to you?"

Her voice cuts straight through the others, as it always does. The sound is not the harsh grating of sand against his nerves, after all, but the cool depths meant to soothe it. It is deep, and calming, and fluid. Her voice sounds how he imagines death might feel.

"Can you truly not hear them?"

His own voice is a dying, wretched thing. He came here to talk with her, but now he is surprised that he can manage even that. His mouth is drier than the sand, and each syllable that falls from between his lips emerges bruised from his efforts.

He glances her way, only to be warded off by the ink black orbs of her piercing eyes still turned his way. They are ugly, terrible eyes.

When she speaks again, it is not a question. "Tell me what they say to you."

He lets out a pathetic sigh, and the others take his weakness as a sign to resume. The winds sing their chorus once more.

"Do not tell her."
"She will not understand."
"Come to us."
"You deserve it."
"Jump."

They do not offer advice that the man dares to take. He is made more uncomfortable by how sweet the idea sounds, but he will not give in, solely for the sake of the creature at his side. He knows she does not wish for him to do it.

"They want me to end it," he says.

The harpies hiss their disapproval of his cowardice. He could have made it. He could have jumped.

"It?" She asks.

"My life," he tells her.

There is a silence between them so solid that even her sisters dare not break it in this moment.

"You would do that?" She asks.

"No," he says quickly.

Perhaps he says it a little too quickly, for the way she bristles after.

"You're lying," she whispers.

How can a voice as eternally deep as her own, still sound so innocent? It is the voice a wounded songbird, and it breaks his heart.

"I would not do that to you."

"You promised!" She shrieks. He cannot help but to flinch under her fury.

He wants to protect her. To comfort her. And yet she terrifies him.

"I know. I know I promised. I would not do it."

He would not wish to do anything that would harm her. Or that would turn her wrath upon him. The rest of them, perhaps, but he would not hurt her.

"You would," she insists. "You were thinking about it. Even now."

He cannot lie to her.

He has been thinking about it more and more.

"I would not jump," he says again. "It is only..."

The moment she takes those eyes off of him, he has the freedom to breathe once more. The air burns bitterly cold as it scrapes across the inside of his lungs. But with her gaze no longer upon him, he knows he does not need to fear the winds. She will let him have what little breath he still requires.

This storm, at least, has passed.

The accusation has drifted away to pain. Her dark curls form a curtain over her face that obscures it from view, but she is once more the loveliest creature in the world to him. Her large wings curl in around her body to brace herself, to shield herself from his answer before she has even posed the question.

"It is only what?"

He has a tough time tearing his eyes from her, and back to the scene below so he might find the words. The sand is as colorless and lifeless as the rocky cliff where the two of them are now perched. The ground is as gray as the sky above, the world all one note. Flat. It is desolate. It is cold.

The island had not been like this when he arrived. He is starting to forget what it had been like instead. Each hour, it seems he loses more and more of himself to hunger.

"I shall die anyway," he tells her. "I can hold on, as I have promised. I will not end myself, for you, but neither can I hold on forever. It is only a matter of time."

"Time until what?"

"Until I starve."

"Why do you believe you are starving?"

"I..." his voice trails and the thought is lost to the winds.

Surely, she must know.

He wants to tell her it is her sisters, the others. They turn all food he takes to dust in his mouth, and no mortal may survive on dust alone.

But she must have seen their torments.

Surely, she knows.

He remembers he was trying to tell her something.

Weakly, he finishes the thought before he can forget it again. "...ache."

Ache is the word he chooses. He is proud of how powerful it is, how true. His mind is not as sharp as it once was, but it has found here the right thing to say.

His whole body aches. For nourishment. For rest. For an end.

It had been one thing when his stomach alone had rumbled and agonized, but now it is the entirety of him. It is a deeper pain; subdued, but constant. It is the sensation that can only come when one's body begins to eat itself to keep going. He does not know how much of him is left to be devoured. He only knows that it is becoming harder and harder to climb this cliff each day for their talks.

Soon enough, it will be impossible for him to come meet her at all.

Then he shall truly have nothing left.

"You ache?"

He nods. That, too, is an effort.

"Does it hurt?"

He nods again.

"Tell me what it feels like."

"I do not know how I could describe such a mortal feeling to one such as yourself."

"Try."

At the harpy's command, he has no choice but to try.

"It is like being the moon," he says. "And waiting to see the sunrise."

The silence lingers between them once again as she turns the thought over and over. It is as close as he comes these days to rest, for even his dreams are filled with the faces of her sisters mocking him.

"You are tired," she says in cool understanding.

"I am."

"Do you truly wish for it to end?"

He has to think about it.

There are so many things he wants. Some food. A drink. A proper bed. Perhaps the touch of a lovely creature. But rest, in any form, may well be a welcome comfort.

It is what he wrestles with when the winds sing to him.

"I do not know."

"You do not think it matters."

He shrugs, and this is yet another effort upon his weary body. "I am to die anyway."

He had promised her he would not try to jump, or end things, or take his life back into his own hands while on the island. He can hold on, but only because he knows he will not be able to hold on forever. The end is coming for him; he is certain, as it comes for all men.

Perhaps she is right.

He does not truly believe it matters one way or the other, when his undoing shall be the same.

Her next words chill him with their certainty, their finality.

"You are not to die."

He feels her eyes weigh on him once more, and it is almost enough already to push him over the edge.

He does not answer her.

She does not relent.

"How long do you think it has been since you have eaten?"

He tries to recall.

He has not been counting the days since his imprisonment began, has not ever thought to track his suffering. He knows only that each day here feels like an eternity unto itself.

"I do not know," he confesses.

"Truly? You cannot remember?"

"Truly."

"It has been over ten years."

This time, he has no choice but to look her way. He wishes only to see if she is being honest, a very human instinct of his. It is, of course, impossible to tell. There is nothing but abyss staring back at him from under her lashes. The abyss says naught.

"That cannot be."

"Cannot be, and yet it is."

"I would be dead," he protests.

"And yet..."

She does not need to say the rest, for it is plain enough to see. He is not dead, for he is here still. They are conversing.

"How...?"

"The Gods must not wish for you to die."

There is a strength in his anger that makes him animated once more. It gives his voice volume he had not believed it possible for him to still possess. It is courage enough that he may lash out. "Why would they torture me so, only to give me the favor that I might not perish?"

"Is it a favor they have done you?"

Her words are as cold as her eyes.

He does not know how he has survived this hunger for ten years. He is certain he could not survive it another ten without succumbing to utter madness.

No, he decided. It was not a favor they had done him after all.

"How long shall this go on?"

"Until you starve," she says simply.

Only he knows he will not starve. If he has not already, it is not likely he shall soon waste away to the terrible pain of the sensation. Only now does he feel the true weight of the promise he made to her. The ground calls to him in a ceaseless longing to break it, and to go back on his words. The chorus swells in song at the taste of his panic.

"Only you can end this."

"Go now."

"It will be easy."

"Do it."

"Jump."

"You can, if you want."

This time there is a sixth voice in the song; hers.

"I would not break a promise to you," he says.

He knows he is being tested.

"Have you forgotten what you are being punished for? The promise you have already broken?"

He has.

It's a terrible thing to realize he cannot remember what has earned him such a harsh sentence in the first place. He cannot remember what he has done, or why. Worse still, he cannot remember own name. His mother's face. Where he had come from. The hunger has taken more of him away than he realized. More than he thinks he can bear.

Shakily, he rises to his feet.

She makes no move to stop him.

He looks down to the harpy.

The harpy looks back.

She would be so beautiful, the most beautiful thing in the world, were it not for her eyes. They are the eyes of pure nothingness, of despair. They are enough to turn her visage into something twisted, almost as shriveled and cruel as the faces of her sisters cackling over him in his dreams. Were it not for those eyes, perhaps he could stop himself from breaking the promise.

As he looks to her for guidance, and sees only such terrors as would inflict his nightmares, he does not even find the strength to apologize for his weakness.

He flings himself readily over the edge.

It is sweet relief to see the end in sight as the ground approaches.

Then he is engulfed by the black feathers of her wings.

He does not need to see those terrible eyes to feel the coldness in her. Her talons rake at his flash as she deposits him safely to those icy sands. The pain of such wounds shrieks her anger loud enough in her silence.

He has broken a promise to a harpy, now, the one being that might have ended his torments. No doubt she will increase them now, and he shall have no choice but to endure until he starves.

Revenge Body

♥

THERE ARE THREE WAYS in which a person can burn.

Ally has experienced all three, though she remembers the first only as a distant memory; the peeling of plastic skin off a red, ruined, shell of a person.

There's someone else.

That first way is the sunburn that will continue to scar, even as layer after layer of flesh comes free.

Sweatband's skin does not come off in such a careless manner.

There is no renewal in it, no morbid sense of relief or fascination from the screaming man as he struggles to escape. There is only pain, and noise, and thrashing while she frees his blood from where it has been trapped inside him.

Ally would worry about the noise, but luckily she found him in one of the gym's soundproofed studios. Those had cost her a pretty penny in renovations.

For private classes, you know? It'll be worth it.

Her spoiled, vapid, leech of an ex girlfriend had been right about one point, it seemed. The soundproofing *had* been worth it.

Ally gives one final tug on the strip still in her hand and watches as the flesh gives way, revealing more wet muscle underneath. She waits patiently for him to quiet down as she contemplates.

It's strange to her, this new way of looking at the human form. It's not new, exactly. There are those illustrations in biology textbooks, and she knows that med students would often look at cadavers peeled in a similar manner. But Ally is no doctor in training. She would not have ever imagined getting a front-row seat to this live demonstration of someone's inner workings.

It makes her want to do more peeling.

Instead, she is patient, and the noise does die down.

In waves the gurgling, sobbing stops. Sweatband quits thrashing and squirming from where she has him effortlessly pinned to the floor. When he is down to no more than weak groans, she addresses him.

"Do you know Lena Rollins?" She asks calmly.

She is amazed at how expressive his muffled wail is. There is pain, defeat, pleading, and still somehow a hint of incredulity. He wants to ask her if she means it. If this whole thing is truly about Lena. If she expects him, in his condition, to talk.

Ally admits that she may have gone overboard when she initially overpowered him. She will try not to make that mistake with other.

"Lena Rollins," she repeats. "Do you know her?"

She grabs his hair roughly and her hand squelches in the blood-soaked sweatband she used to tell him apart from the other one that had been lurking around the building during these night hours. This elicits another pained cry. It takes him a minute to recover, but Ally does not need to repeat herself a third time.

His broken jaw hangs open, but she can hear the strained start of vocalization and see the protruding tongue begin to waggle.

"You can just nod," she says, cutting off whatever answer he was trying to give. She even lessens the twisting grip she has on him as a sign of good faith.

It must be agony, but she feels the tug as he nods his head.

"Good." She tells him. She's been worried he would try to lie. "Are you fucking her?"

The surprise in his eyes is subdued through everything else, but it is genuine.

She watches closely to determine if he is surprised at the notion, or at getting caught.

He shakes his head, what little bit he can, from side to side to answer in the negative.

She believes him.

You don't know them.

Her bet honestly, was that it was Sweatband. But half the fun of guessing is in finding out.

She takes a final look over at the muscles of his mangled left arm as the fingers twitch in their exposed agony.

"Then this isn't personal," she assures him, and snaps his neck.

It was true. He'd simply been in the wrong place at the wrong time.

She could have left him in the studio, given him a chance to be found or to claw his way to freedom. But he was suffering, and Ally is not a monster. Not truly.

Not yet.

She stands and wipes her hands on the black Lycra fabric of her pants. A little bit of blood is fine — especially in the dark. Too much, however, would give away the game. She has every intention of playing with the next one, if she can control herself a little longer. She's not sure she can. It feels close.

He's athletic.

There's a faint echo in the gym, outside the little studio bubble. She opens the door and is greeted with the last, trailing "o" of a question called into a darkness that is no longer vacant. It is no longer safe.

She follows the sound to where she knows that Too-Small T-shirt is trapped.

"Hello?" He calls again, and again his tentative voice echoes slightly. She makes sure to stand a good distance back as watches and thinks about how to proceed. It's fun to watch him squirm.

The danger is also enticing. Even though she had savored the last kill immensely, it had been low risk. She knew she'd get away with it. There's a chance, out here in the open, for her plan to unravel near the end. This is no soundproof studio, and the victim is already making noise. There are even windows, though the street is not going to be busy at this time of night. Not until much later.

One could call this recklessness on her part. She prefers to think of it as a fighting chance for her opponent. He is, after all, the underdog.

He plays into the role well while she watches.

When yet another one of his cries goes unanswered, he tests his own ability to release himself. He is tantalizingly careful in his approach to start, and even from this distance she can see the gears turning in his brain. His Adam's apple already brushes against the weight bar each time he swallows — had probably pressed in a bit when he had tried to call for help. He doesn't understand how it can be so low to the ground, on the ground, and yet be so heavy. He doesn't seem to suspect, yet, that the bar has been tampered with. There is a safe distance between him and suffocation, but Ally does hope to see some rising panic over that idea.

His arms fold up, she imagines not for the first time since he's awakened there, and his hands curl around the bar. The dark gray fabric of his undersized T-shirt stretches tighter across his straining bicep muscles as he tests the weight.

He knows it's too heavy.

He is realizing, or perhaps reaffirming, that it would be too much for him to lift off of himself — especially in this position. The floor does not offer the same kinetic benefits as the weight bench.

If he tries and fails, he could tear a muscle. He could sprain a wrist. He could drop that bar on himself. None of that would help his situation.

Yet the longer he stays he stays here, the more embarrassing it will be when he is found. She thinks he might be thinking about this as he tries to pull himself free, bumping the bar first with his chest, then with his chin. Then again, more frantically with his chest, as if he can squirm his way free. As if he hasn't been working hard on the muscles that are now trapping him.

Maybe the tickle of the weight bar is starting to bother him, because he puts his hands back and tries again to lift.

He strains hard.

Ally can see the veins in his arm bulging. He would not be trying this hard if he were still just testing. His breathing would not be so heavy if he were just trying to gather intel on how stuck he truly was. The bar moves a bit, rocks ever so slightly on the weights that hold it off his neck. It's not enough. T-shirt redoubles his efforts and keeps trying fruitlessly despite the burning of his muscles.

Yes, this is the second kind of burn.

It is the sweet aching of the final rep, the constant reminder of hard work. It is the melting away of weakness, and the body's acceptance of inevitable change.

At first, that sensation had been a deterrent to Ally. She could not distinguish between the fires. The burning of her skin had been a harsh lesson in limitations. Why should the burning of her muscles be any different?

But it was. Once she got to know that second, pleasurable burn, it had become the sweetest lover she had ever known. She'd reveled in the warm destruction of who she had once been.

The old Ally had been addicted to comfort.

She'd found success early in life. She had a job where she could work from her nice home. She had wealth to share with the woman of her dreams. She had grown complacent in her happiness. As Lena had put it, she had grown soft.

I want someone who tries a little harder.

The new Ally tried.

Perhaps she tried too hard, for eventually, that sweet ache of her muscles had become more evasive. There was no feeling left to chase.

Yet here, now, she sees her victim experiencing it. Another sweet thing he has that she doesn't — if he truly is the other person Lena had mentioned. When she thinks about it that way, red begins to creep into the corners of her vision.

Why must everything that felt good leave her for the sake of this stranger?

Everything about him drives her insane.

His struggling form, the little grunts he makes, his attire.

Had he thought the T-shirt would make his muscles look bigger? Ally thinks it makes him appear like an overgrown man child who doesn't know how to dress himself. With the way Lena had spoken about her new partner, Ally has been waiting to be impressed.

She is anything but.

"This can't be him," she mutters.

She thinks it's under her breath, but suddenly his straining stops.

"Hello?" He calls again. Then, "Lena?"

In that one question, he gives himself away. It is not the cry of a coworker hoping for his manager to save him. It is the insecure whine of a person who thinks the woman he stole is about to see him for the pathetic mess he is.

Ally knows what must be done.

She steps from the darkness and into his line of sight. She's illuminated well enough by what city light filters in through the windows at this hour. Perhaps there will be a witness to cut her fun short, but she doesn't think so.

Too-Small T-Shirt squints up at her, and then his eyes go wide. There is something in them she had not expected to encounter from her nameless foe; recognition.

"Ally?"

She tries to recall where she has seen him before, but she hasn't. She knows the gym, and its staff well from the days before the horrid beach vacation break-up. The old Ally wanted to keep tabs on her investment with the love of her life.

The red darkens in her eyes.

Lena must have told him about her. Probably when they were still together.

Ally could imagine her ex explaining that soon, she'd be single soon, they could go public then, but she had to wait until everything was paid for or she could be on the financial hook for her dream business.

"You look different."

She would be flattered by the awe in his expression, were she not so painfully angered by the familiar tone in his voice, like they're friends. Like he didn't take everything from her.

"I've been working out," she says, but it's not her voice so much as what it is a hollow growl.

She is having difficulty seeing anything past crimson hues.

It's almost time.

He laughs. He's uncomfortable, and so he laughs. "That's one hell of a revenge body."

Ally laughs too. Something about the tabloid style term strikes her as incomprehensibly funny.

The men at the gym she's been training at secretly told her she was going about it wrong if she wanted to lose weight. They thought it was about being pretty. About winning someone back.

T-shirt had gotten it in one. It's about revenge.

Now that he's as good as acknowledging his role in her misfortune, there's little point in dragging it out and that makes her laugh even harder with relief. Right when she thought she'd be missing out. The vermillion scene before her throbs in time to her pulse.

"What's so—"

She doesn't have the time left to let him finish.

She stomps down, hard, between his legs and the question is cut short by his own wheezing groan of pain. It's enough to distract him while she bends down to pick up one of his legs.

"Please," he mouths — that's what she thinks he's saying — and then *crack!*

His knee is bending the wrong way, his sneaker hanging up over the bar that traps him.

He finds the air he was lacking to scream properly.

The sound is animalistic, and it carries well through the building. It's the sort of sound that she's sure Lena is hearing over whatever Top 40 shit she's playing in her office right now. It is the signaling cry that Ally needs and she bends his other leg up over the bar like a pretzel too to keep him singing.

He may be suffering more, but it is Ally who begins to bleed.

Her skin peels.

Her muscles ache.

It all goes red.

Her body finishes its ascension just in time to hear the footsteps rushing toward her.

She is experiencing the ecstasy of the third, and final burn — the kind that can twist a human up into a monster.

Ramen of Regret

♥

The good news is that it's hard to screw this one up. You need that right now. You don't know what the hell you're doing.

Ingredients:

1 package of noodles
Chicken/beef broth
Chili powder
2 eggs
Veggies of your preference
MEAT

Step 1. Soft boil eggs. Think about all the trips to Asia you wanted to take and didn't. The places you wanted to eat, and were told no. Realize the eggs are now hard boiled. Peel them and slice them in half anyway. It's fine.

Step 2. Boil the chicken/beef broth. A better wife might have homemade stock in the freezer. You likely have a carton or a can, or a powdered packet. Maybe a little foil-wrapped cube? You may as well be making instant ramen at this point, but it's fine. It's *expected*.

Step 3. This is the step that matters. Put in the chili powder. So much chili powder. You want it to *burn*. The broth should be as red as your hands. The steam should make your eyes water. You want to forget how his lips tasted right before... well... let's just say you want to forget.

Step 4. Mix in those noodles.

Step 5. Cut the veggies. Not onions. Never onions. *He* liked onions, and you have enough regrets without thinking about *him* right now. There are better things to think about. The classes you quit. The women you lusted after, but never kissed.

You think you might be bi. Maybe pan. You're not sure you understand the difference. You never got that chance to explore because you were already married (to a man) when you dropped out of college. But no. Don't think about that yet. Just put the veggies into the broth.

Step 6. Now you may finally wonder about your life choices. Really let it all sink in as the noodles get done, maybe a little overdone and soft. Flavor them with the salt of your tears. This is the meal you *deserve*.

Step 7. Pour the disappointing, mushy noodles into a bowl. Garnish with eggs that are a little too hard boiled. Try to stir the veggies to the top for some aesthetically pleasing splashes of color, even though it's too late to make this look good.

Step 8: Finish with one thick cut of MEAT.

If you had gone Asia like you wanted, this could be ham or beef. You can use whatever kind you have on hand, but we highly recommend a red, raw, fresh cut from the MEAT lying in your kitchen floor.

Really *taste* that regret.

Twelve Hour Lifespan

♥

6:00 PM

The fly has only this one day to live and cannot wait for it to be over. It lies on the same soiled sheets where it crashed and tries to ignore its suffering long enough for the sun to set on its time left upon the Earth.

The little creature, mangled as it is, and already accustomed to filth, still finds that it is disgusted by the surroundings. The apartment is sweltering and filled with the sickening stench of sweat. It is a horrid, and lonely place to die.

What a thing, for a lowly insect to be so filled with human regret. Yet the fly would do it all differently if it could. It would have fought the urge to return to this hovel. It would have stayed in the bunker, where all its best hours had been spent. It would choose now, if it could, to be surrounded by others — and damn them if they were revolted by its appearance. In lack of that, all the fly can hope for is to sleep until this tremendous pain has stopped.

Until everything has stopped.

It is nearing the end of the hour when the fly is roused once more by a scream. The sound reaches something deep and forgotten inside the insect, which can do naught to help, but is compelled to the window all the same.

The poor thing has no wings left to carry it over. It crawls from the bed and teeters precariously on its two remaining legs, feeling heavy and misshapen. It leans on the glass to peer out over the empty street below.

The screaming is gone. Whoever made it is instantly forgotten. All that matters now is the blinding light that consumes the world.

In the fly's final moments, it mistakes the end for a sunset. It is grateful to be staring at something so beautiful when it goes.

5:00 PM

The crash is brutal.

The mattress the fly lands on is soft enough, but that is of little consequence. The journey home and the harrowing arrival have taken more from the insect than it ever had to give.

Its legs crumple up beneath it, and tangled still they are crushed beneath the weight of its body. The overexerted wings fall dormant, too thin and tired to move. They stick where they land, plastered to the damp fabric.

The creature twists and kicks in its panic, and fights until it feels the fibrous membranes rip from its back.

A fly that cannot fly.

The realization sinks in most painfully to the pathetic creature, who doesn't understand how it can be so useless and have so much body left.

It cannot even remember why it had been so intent to return to this wretched bed where it had been born.

4:00 PM

The fly is weary, but it squeezes itself through the space under the door, eager to be home.

It has a message for the man who lives here.

Only there is no man.

It flits around, to the tiny kitchen, to the filthy bathroom, looking for any sign of his maker.

The hope drains from it as the panic rises and thoughts become harder and harder to grasp.

There was supposed to be someone here.

There was supposed to be a human man to return to.

It was supposed to feel like home.

The fly had something important to say

It's not a conscious decision that the insect makes to give up. Eventually, the little body is just too exhausted to keep looking.

3:00 PM

The streets have changed drastically since this morning. There is no one to hitch a ride on, and the fly is not as young as it was in the hours before noon. It has to travel against the wind, tired and alone.

The world seems largely deserted now.

There are a handful of people, scared and scattered in the little recesses between buildings. Human leftovers.

They have nowhere better to be, no hope for the future, and no one they want to spend their final night with, if the rumors about the end are to be believed.

It is a desolate, and disheartening sight that slows the journey.

But the fly persists.

It is different from these others. It does have somewhere important to be.

2:00 PM

The tall man near the door is the last person in the bunker to share his story.

From the wall, the fly watches.

"I'm Colton," he says.

The room is silent for him, save for the sniffling and heavy breathing, interspersed with occasional coughs.

"There's not much of a story," he says, but in a strained way that hints at the truth. "I'm just someone that wants to be alive tomorrow."

There's a pause.

Some of the others had struggled to share as well. But everyone down there had something to get off their chests. Colton is no different in that regard. In a startling display of human compassion, the audience is patient.

"My... p*artner*," he chooses the word carefully. He is a cautious and prudent man, in a dangerous situation. He does not wish to reveal too much. "I wanted to bring them. But they wouldn't come."

This is met with more silence.

"I begged. For a week. Ever since I knew this place would be open. But they wouldn't come. This morning... I almost didn't leave. A better man would have stayed, I think." He shrugs, as though it can hide the moisture in his eyes. "But I wanted to live. So here I am."

The fly realizes why it's here.

What its purpose is.

There's someone at home who should want to live as well.

1:00 PM

"I'm Sim," says the boy that kicks off the last full hour of tragic tales. The fly has settled in comfortably at this point, for even the most restless in the crowd have stopped trying to swat at it. "It's just me," he continues. "My family left the city a couple days ago."

It's obvious from his dejected tone that he had either not been invited, or had not felt welcomed.

"We've been fighting," he explains. "For a couple months now. I just wanted them to see me for who I am. And they kept telling me there was bigger stuff going on in the world right now than how I felt or what I called myself. They just wanted to focus on, you know." he gestures around.

All the humans in the room seem to understand. They have all been through big things in the last several weeks.

"I blame myself a little. Maybe I shouldn't have pushed it. But, I felt that if I didn't do it now, I never would. And I didn't want to die pretending I was something I'm not."

This part, the fly understands.

It knows a thing or two about pretending.

12:00 PM

"I'm Addison," offers the woman with the big belly.

The fly is only half paying attention when she starts her tale, because there is a big man by the wall with arms long enough to graze the insect if he so chose.

"I've been living here all my life, but I just got my own apartment a couple months ago. It's pretty nice, considering. I wanted to be ready for the baby."

She puts her hands over her stomach protectively.

The fly thinks this is a very grim way to start the hour. If the rumors are true, and the end is coming, it seems like a terrible time to bring life into the world.

Spirits in the bunker seem to lift at her words, however. There is something so human about the idea of life carrying on.

It seems incomprehensible to so small and disconnected a creature as the fly.

11:00 AM

At almost exactly 11:00, a child breaks the thick silence that has settled underground.

"I'm Lulu."

The young woman holding her hand — a mother, or perhaps an older sister — pulls her closer. "Lulu, hush."

"Daddy always said that when you were scared, you could count on your friends to help. But we don't have any friends here."

"I'm sorry, everyone." Says the woman.

The little girl begins to cry. "I'm just trying to make some new friends."

She's scared. One by one, people begin speaking up to introduce themselves so that the little girl is not so alone.

They stop being a faceless mob, and the whole thing becomes very real, where before it had been but a figment.

The fly wants to get lost in these stories for as long as they continue to offer a distraction from reality. But the truth is, there's only one person in the room it actually wants to hear from.

There's only one story here that matters.

10:00 AM

Being in the bunker is not unlike being in the subway.

Or dreaming of being in the subway.

There is a certain sense of claustrophobia. The people are sitting uncomfortably close to countless strangers.

None of them seem to have faces. Or voices of their own. The silence is not absolute, broken as it is by indeterminate whispers that muffle one another and may as well be in a foreign language.

The thing wants nothing to be more than a proverbial fly on the wall, observing unnoticed.

But the longer the uncomfortable silence lingers, the more it feels like the eyes of the crowd are upon him.

The more hands come up to swat at it. One grazes a now bruised wing.

The more distracted the insect becomes, the less attention it can pay to its reason for being here.

9:00 AM

The first thing that the fly notices about the "bunker" is that it is not airtight.

It hopes that it's wrong in how the scene presents itself. But there are cracks in the wall, and there is space under the door to escape through even once the place is sealed. Whatever the room had been built for initially, it must have seen better days.

It's sturdy enough still, that it may well survive a small blast. If there is any kind of accompanying radiation, however, the inhabitants of will be nothing more than soup by tomorrow.

The fly would be upset by this image, but there is a certain comforting freedom in knowing that it will not, under any circumstances, have a tomorrow. It will not see what is left of these strangers come the dawn.

Still, the fly feels a little bad. Despite itself, it worries for Colton.

This is a terrible, selfish human man. He has done terrible, selfish things as recent as this morning. If the insect were taking things personally, it would say that he *deserved* to be irradiated and maybe liquefied with the others.

But flies, it reasoned, don't have feelings strong enough to wish a violent death on the handsome man standing in a scary place, looking so alone.

8:00 AM

The streets are chaos.

Glass is broken, shops and establishments are open and emptied to the world of rioters.

There is not as much violence on the streets as is being reported, but only for the sake that the city's citizens are moving with a purpose.

Many of them believe.

Those who do not believe were moved by the collective madness of those who do. Damn the consequences they may never live to see.

The fly is overwhelmed to the point of near indifference. In the cacophony, it doesn't know where to go. It knows only the vague direction of its destination, and has never travelled so far before — being less than a full hour old at this point in its life.

By luck, or fortune, or the selfish design of the fly's creator, it sees someone it recognized at the end of that first block.

There is a deep sense of longing in the insect as it sees the man standing there, on broken glass, stationary in a moving sea of other humans. He is looking at the broken window of what had been his favorite cafe.

He would not have thought the establishment was important to him, but seeing it shattered seems to resonate with the man. A part of his life, a stable part of his life, is now broken, and things will never be the same.

The fly lands on his back while he lets himself work through the feelings. Uncertain if he was right or not, he takes a deep breath and carries them both forward.

7:00 AM

Max lays in his bed, aware that the world may be ending, but not in a state of mind to care. If anything, he wishes it would hurry up so that he doesn't have to worry about getting up for food or water.

He knows his apartment is disgusting, and that he in particular is filthy. It hardly seems to matter, in light of the bigger things that have already happened today.

He thinks about chasing after Colton, but he doesn't

His boyfriend — ex-boyfriend — must not have loved him so terribly after all, to leave him all alone. For that matter, Max isn't sure that he's capable of loving someone who was capable of leaving him all alone.

There is a faint spark of irritation, which is as close as he can muster to anger. He tries to hold on to the feeling. He'd been wronged. Surely, a righteous fury such as this would be a better way to spend his final day than just more of the same numbness that has been slowly drowning him.

He tries and fails to work himself into a passion over the sudden breakup.

It doesn't help that he couldn't picture what a proper revenge would look like. What can he possibly do at this late in the game to prove Colton wrong?

Pick up the place? Clean himself? Find some stupid, frivolous way to pretend he's enjoying himself during the end of days? It sounds pointless, and not worth the effort, and quickly Max's interest in the idea dwindles back down into nothing.

He isn't even sure he believes all the doomsayer, end of the world shit anyway.

To be quite honest, he doesn't care.

He tries to fall back asleep, but their last conversation keeps plaguing his thoughts with nothing to distract him.

"I figured you'd rather sleep through it," Colton had said when Max had caught him trying to sneak out.

It hurt more because it had been true.

The fight had been short, but nasty, filled with more truths to cut what was left of Max to the bone.

"All you want to do anymore is sleep."

"You won't even try."

"We can get you more medication after this is over, but not if we're dead."

"I can't do this anymore."

"You just want to be a fucking fly on the wall, watching humanity's destruction."

That last, desperate metaphor really stuck with him.

Max doesn't know a lot about flies, but that they are seen as insignificant, vile little things, attracted to the filth of the world. That is how exactly how he himself feels, these days.

There's some breed of fly, he's pretty sure, that only lives for twenty-four hours. He doesn't think that is the same kind of house-fly he's picturing becoming in his head as a distraction, but that hardly matters.

The lifespan of every living creature on the planet is, from this moment forward, about twelve hours.

Not Like Lettie

♥

Part 1: The Choosing

The other girls looked to Lettie with relief when it was time to begin The Choosing. There were rules and safeguards against behaving poorly to avoid drinking from the chalice, but there was no rule made by man or god that could make the average school girl as pure as *her*.

For that one day, for the first time, they were all grateful.

Those who had looked at her with jealousy and resentment on countless occasions before could all breathe a collective sigh of relief, even when Father Wilford stepped inside the circle. They were all happy to forfeit any and all attention for this one event. They kept their silence as he walked from girl to girl, appraising them, and saying his silent prayers before each of them in turn.

The only one unsure of the outcome was, of course, Lettie herself. Pride was a sin, but it was not a willing ignorance on her part, or even an attempt to shun such pride. No, it was not the absence of a sin that made her blind to the inevitable, but rather the presence of another virtue.

Lettie Engels saw the best in everyone.

Juniper, who had been known to steal treats from the kitchens, had also nursed many a fallen sparrow back to health.

Iris, who feigned ill to avoid both chores and lessons, had the loveliest singing voice in the whole choir.

Rosemary, who knew all the swears, could calm anyone down in an emergency, even if they had been hurt.

Even Daisy, who was cruel and selfish, and liked to torment and tease the other children, would say her prayers to the Mother each night without ever once needing to be reminded.

Through Lettie's eyes, each one of them was worthy of being chosen. Each of them was Good Blood and fitting to feel the Mother's embrace. It was this spirit of acceptance that made Father Wilford present the chalice to Lettie once his prayers had been concluded.

It was customary for girls to cry once they had been chosen. Not all honors felt worth having in the moment they are to be bestowed. Though a girl may strive for eight, or twelve, or in Lettie's case fifteen years to be the one selected, she might still feel sorrow when the moment came to pass. Tears, worried looks, and shaky pleas were all things to be expected. In the girl's final hours, they were undoubtedly forgiven.

There was only a smile on Lettie's lips, however, as she took the chalice into her hands and drank deep of its mercy. No one had ever seen her look quite so happy.

She had no cause for doubt that she could see. All her life she'd heard the stories of what an honor it would be to feed the earth, and how she should do her best to try and be Good Blood. There was no greater possible mark of her success than to be chosen. She had seen all her years how their community struggled, and was happy to play her part in bringing them a decent harvest at long last.

So she drank without hesitation until the last drop had been swallowed.

No one dared speak during this most sacred of tasks, but there was rustling. There was palpable discomfort.

It was one thing to send a girl to the grave who grasps the unfairness that is being done to her. It was another thing entirely to send one who seemed so eager to go. It was akin to playing a cruel trick, one from which even Daisy shied away.

It was bad.

Whenever a part of the process felt amiss, there was a lingering sense of tension. The girls could at any moment learn to begrudge their sacrifice. They could learn to ask questions. They could begin to unravel the fabric of the community.

To Lettie, at least, the ritual still felt the most natural thing in the world.

The wine tasted of blackberries, which had always been her favorite. The taste lingered, rich and thick on her tongue, and was all she could think of as her legs began to give out.

Sweet, she thought. *I have never tasted anything so sweet.*

The two men behind her were quick to catch her, and to make her descent onto the damp ground as peaceful as possible. If her fall was smooth, perhaps the rest of the ceremony could follow suit.

She lay on her back with her arms outstretched and her red hair fanned beneath her. She looked up at the stars, her green eyes wide with wonder.

She had been told this was the part where the earth was supposed to swallow her up from below, but the wine made it seem as though the opposite was happening. She was actually rising up, out of her body, and able to look down upon herself.

It was a familiar dream, one she'd had many times but had never dared to repeat aloud. She was grateful to have been chosen and relieved that her deepest desire had finally come to pass. It was just like she had always imagined it.

Part 2: The Mother's Embrace

> "And the Mother, in her eternal grace, provides for us. As she feeds us, so must we feed her. Seeds are sown into the ground, and it is up to us to water them.
>
> "The Mother requests only that the blood be good, and ripened for such sacrifice. By choosing only the worthy, and choosing well, we ensure that our people will be provided for.
>
> "Those who go into the ground to feed the earth shall be only those who have been chosen carefully. Only those with the Good Blood shall be eligible for

> such an honor, as they are about to become one with the Mother.
>
> "When the last drop has fallen from their veins, they shall be swallowed by the ground where they lie. At such a time, their mortal pain shall be finished. In that hour of darkness, the Mother shall accept them into her eternal embrace, to bring them such mercy as they have earned."

And the Mother came to Lettie, but her embrace was not eternal after all.

Part 3: The Chosen

If Judah had been uncomfortable about the island's practices before, it was nothing compared to how he felt once he saw the body of the child hit the grass.

She was smiling, still.

Why does that make it so much worse?

Her whole-hearted participation in the ritual had unnerved him greatly. The look of utter innocence on her young face had broken him in ways that he, a man grown, still could not fathom.

What sort of life did my father leave to me?

Judah had not known much of his father. His mother had spoken of him seldom, and with distaste. Now, more than ever, Judah was beginning to understand why. Had she come from this wretched place? From this cult? Was she a survivor? An escapee?

He didn't find it likely that it should be the case. It was difficult for him to imagine the stern, no nonsense woman who had raised him, growing up in a blood harvest cult. Then again, she had taught him all she'd known about common sense, and he had still found himself in a position to witness the murder of a child.

Sacrifice.

That was the word. The magical, biblical, word that was supposed to make it all okay.

That smile, though.

He shuddered and waited for the prayers to be done.

I will leave, he thought. *I will be on the first ship out of here tomorrow.*

That was just an expression. It was not as though there were many ships that came and went from the island — remote as it was. 'Island' was just an expression, also.

The village was actually settled on a peninsula, but had been referring to itself as an island by generations of residents with no intention to ever leave. For them, it may as well have been an island, secluded and private, and entirely cut off by water from the rest of the world. For Judah, though, there was some small inkling of hope to be gleaned from this little fact.

The path to the mainland may be steep and overgrown, but he could always travel on foot if he absolutely had to. He was not as isolated as the villagers would have him believe. It left him another option to escape such madness.

Tomorrow, he promised himself. *Tomorrow.*

For now, it would have to be enough that he stood silently with Father Wilford and did not arouse any suspicion that he meant to leave.

The men of the island, typically, seemed to be in less danger than their female counterparts. The terrible traditions seemed to target exclusively the fairer sex, and Judah was not so blind as to think it a coincidence. Neither was he naïve enough to believe that such archaic ways should extend far enough as to protect him, if he was caught dissenting.

Family or not, blood or not, he was still an outsider to these people. He was still a threat. Even he did not truly know what he meant to do with the information he had gathered once he could get it off the little curve of land. For that reason, and for so many others, he knew he must continue with the utmost caution.

He had seen what they could do.

So he waited.

The outer circle made their departure first. These were largely the women of the community, old enough to have survived their own Choosings, and now exercising their right to witness. They were accompanied by the children, boys and girls alike, who were meant to learn the meaning of such selflessness.

Men were not allowed on the field on the night of the Choosing, save for the spiritual leader and an apprentice such as he saw fit to bring. That meant Father Wilford, and tonight, Judah.

He tried to believe that it was a blessing bestowed upon him that he had been a firsthand witness to something that may finally bring him to his senses. More than that, he believed he was cursed for not taking some chance to intervene.

He would tell himself, he realized, for years to come, that he would have been powerless to stop such a thing. The girl had not resisted her fate, which had long since been decided. To meddle would have been to sign his own death warrant, and still she would have died. He was alone, outnumbered, and surrounded by fanatics. It would not have ended well-to-do anything but the nothing that he had done. Into his old age, Judah would tell himself that to know his own limitations had been a moment of prudence; not cowardice.

He would always bear the bitter weight of the truth, however, which was that he had not even thought to do anything until after she was already upon the ground.

The inner circle was to leave next. They consisted of the four girls who had not been chosen. Three looked to be the dead girl's juniors by only a handful of years, but the youngest could not have been more than nine.

Judah's stomach roiled to think of it.

They had chanted their words with Father Wilford as their chosen had slipped away, but now it was time for them to say their silent prayers before departure. They bowed their heads over the body for several more minutes that they might commune with the Mother.

Judah shifted uncomfortably, but Father Wilford looked at ease. It may be another standard part of the procedure, but it could not end soon enough.

The girls concluded, all four at the same time, and filed out counterclockwise around the body.

Tonight, Judah promised himself again. He did not see how he could stand to wait until the morning, and he dared not try to sleep, for fear that he might dream of the child's smile.

Father Wilford bowed his head as the girls trailed over the hill and out of sight.

He held the position for a long time.

Judah did not want to watch him, but neither could he stand to look at the body of the dead girl any longer. It felt like a test of his patience, and one that he was on the verge of failing before the Father finally spoke up.

"She really is a chosen one, you know."

The reverence in his voice was different from the deep, performative kind he usually spoke with.

"Are they not all chosen ones?"

Is that not the point?

Father Wilford just shook his head. "Not like her. Not like Lettie."

Judah felt a chill creeping up his body, from his feet through his very core. He shivered despite the warm weather of the fading summer season. "How then?"

"Each year we do the best we can. We offer up the best we have so that the Mother might have her fill of Good Blood. But many years, the last several at least, the blood has been spoilt. Years of drought and strife has caused a great suffering in the community. I fear it has much weakened the faith of our people."

He believes, Judah realizes. *He truly believes.*

It was enough to scare him. That sincere, infectious sort of belief was what had gotten him to follow along to this point as easily as he had. It was the unbridled faith that promised the ends would always justify the means, no matter how dark those means became along the way. Judah did not think he was immune to further succumbing to the poison of such notions, and he knew he ought to proceed with further caution.

All the same, he asked. "So you believe Lettie was different?"

It felt wrong to say her name.

"I know she is."

He did not like that the answer was given in the present tense.

"I hope so," is all he said. It would be a shame if that brave child had given up her life so willingly to a false god. Hope, though, was a slippery thing. To hope that Lettie had been truly chosen by a higher power would be to hope also that such a power existed. That, too, would be justification for what he had witnessed. Perhaps then it was better — even for Lettie — if the entire thing was bullshit.

"Help me with her."

Judah looked to Father Wilford, who was looking back at him expectantly.

"What?"

"Her legs," said the Father. "Grab them."

Touching her felt a million times more real than watching her die had done. He expected the skin to feel like ice, as though she was the very source of his chill. She was still warm, however, like she was only sleeping.

Judah took hold of her ankles, Father Wilford her wrists, and she swayed between them as they made the journey to the old shed back behind the church.

Part 4: The Good Blood

Father Wilford clapped the young man on the back. The lad had some of his father's looks about him, underneath his mother's craven tenderness.

He had done quite well with his first Choosing.

"You are a good man, Judah," he assured him. "I know that the Mother sees it as well."

The coward would keep his doubts to himself, the pious man would confess. Father Wilford was vindicated in his high opinion of the man, who confronted his issue aloud. "I do not know that I feel like a good man, after all I have just seen."

"To doubt is to care. I implore you, when you make it back to your cabin, pray upon it."

"I will."

"And Judah?"

"Yes?"

"Thank you for your help tonight. Your father would be proud."

Judah opened his mouth, then closed it. He merely responded with a polite bow of his head. His faith, no doubt, would falter, but Father Wilford had a good feeling he would come around eventually to land on the right side of things. It bode well that he'd shown up in time to see the Engels child get chosen.

He had almost insisted that Judah stay to witness the real miracle of the night, as his father had done so many times before. He had feared, however, that it was as likely to push the son away as what it was likely to bring him into the fold.

When he was alone, and the door had creaked to a close, Father Wilford turned around and was surprised to see that Lettie was already awake.

She truly was something spectacular, a creature like no other.

Her reaction during the ceremony had been an extraordinary thing, but it was nothing compared to this. She was bound on the same altar as those who had come before, but she seemed to suffer none of their confusion or panic. She did not struggle or question or beg, and her green eyes shone with clarity.

Still, he felt he owed her at least as much explanation as he had given to her predecessors.

"It is our little secret," he said. "Between me and the women who are chosen."

"Women?" Asked the girl of fifteen, who had been the oldest in many years.

"You have all had your blood, which makes you women in the eyes of the Mother. All of you."

"Thirty-six," she whispered softly.

"What was that?"

"You have shared this secret with thirty-six chosen *girls.*"

Father Wilford was taken aback by this knowledge. Even he did not know the number so precisely. He had not thought to continue counting them after a while. He had been a young man when Father Michael had passed the torch to him, and that may well have been thirty-six years passed. Even so, it was not the sort of thing this girl should have known, or even a thing he could confirm with certainty.

Instead, he steered the conversation as best he could back to where he thought it should be going. "Do you have any questions for me?"

"No."

"I want you to understand that what is about to happen is not a punishment, Lettie. You are still being honored. You are still chosen."

"It will be a punishment, Father."

She did not twist or squirm in her ropes. She just turned to meet his eyes, and somehow this was the most accurate strike she could have made. The green pools in her face were deep, and dark, and wise beyond their years.

"This is how it must be done. The earth must taste your blood."

"Saints and sinners have no hold upon the realm of mortal man. But the Good Blood might yet feed the earth."

"You have the best blood, Lettie."

"Yet yours is worthier of being spilled."

"You are speaking nonsense, child."

She spoke it with such certainty, that the Father was beginning to have his own doubts. Even the girls who'd been present enough of mind to quote scripture before had sounded desperate, and pleading, and not half so sure.

"I speak nonsense, and yet you have done nothing to silence me. I am not gagged."

A chill went through him. "Why would you —"

"Father Michael taught you to gag us so we could not speak. You were to say the prayers and slit our throats quickly. You were not to interact past that."

It was impossible for her to know such a thing. No one had ever known that but him.

"How—"

"Only you have never done it, as he showed you."

"I prefer to give you answers. To offer explanation. It is a final kindness."

"You like to hear them beg."

"No." He shook his head.

"You like to hear us scream."

"You don't know what you're talking about."

"Of course I do," she tilted her head to one side. "Mother told me."

Prayers be damned. Ceremony be damned. Father Wilford reached for the ceremonial dagger to plunge into the girl's heart, that she might be silent once more.

Part 5: The Secret

What Judah had seen in the shed spurred him into more decisive action.

This was a small village, whose residents were not fighters; there was no militia of which to speak. There may be dangers, yes, but it was not a fortress and Judah no longer had the patience required to bide his time. He had listened to the chanting, to the hymnals, to the sermons — and even when the ritual had come into focus, he'd been given the impression that the girl's death would at least be peaceful. The prayers had said she would drink of the ceremonial wine and would be swallowed up by the earth.

Stupid, he chided himself. *Stupid, stupid.*

That was not how anything worked.

Now he was almost certain that she had been alive when he had helped bind her by the wrists and ankles to the stone altar in the shed. He was also sure Father Wilford would have had enough time to carry out her murder by the time he walked past the old building once again.

He'd have sooner avoided that place — especially while it was still inhabited. It could not be helped, though, not if he was going to make good on his word to get the hell out of there that night.

If Father Wilford catches me, he thought, *I will tell him that I prayed on it, and I need to commune further with nature, as the Mother instructed me.*

He did not know if this was something that the Mother would ever say, or if it was something the religion had any precedent for, but he was determined that if he said it with enough conviction, it would have to do.

And if I hear her screaming?

Judah told himself that the best thing he could do for the girl, for *all* the girls of the island, was to get the hell out of there and find help. Still, he did not know if he could be complicit in her death a third time over.

He feared her scream so much that his steps slowed against his will as he started to pass the church.

He froze as the shed door swung open.

A red-headed girl in a bloodstained white dress stepped forward and turned, easing the old door closed so that it would not creak. Her mouth was red when she looked back around to Judah, and she was wearing a wide grin.

She held one finger up to her lips and pursed them into a silent "shhh."

Just like that, she had sworn him to secrecy. It was the least that he owed to the girl, or to whatever had come over her.

He made good on both promises, to flee the island and to keep silent. Judah never told a soul what he had witnessed that night — any of it. He would not tell them even when he woke screaming, from the smile that haunted his dreams each night, for every night after that.

The harvests were good on the island for many years to come, the earth at long last sated from the blood that had been spilled.

Revenir

They say the best revenge is to live well.

Camille had found that to be undeniably true, though the adage had proven hard to follow at first. Rage had been the only thing to pull her from the literal gutter where John had left her. She'd risen from a puddle in the icy rain, wanting nothing more than to warm herself with his blood.

He had shed enough of hers, after all. It only seemed fair.

It was only the beauty of the night that had saved her from seeking immediate satisfaction. Clouds had hidden all the sky. The storm must have knocked out power, for there had been no streetlights to illuminate the grisly state she'd been in. It was the city as she'd never seen it, pitch black and yet completely clear.

She'd seen that night what rock bottom must surely look like, yet she had never felt better a day in her life. That sense of immense power coursing through her in the serene setting, it was like a drug. She wanted more of it, more of everything, to make more of her life this time around. Getting even was something to be savored, and that was what had sent her home.

Tonight, she meant to see if it was worth the wait.

"This piece is very challenging," pondered the critic aloud. The old Camille would have wondered if 'challenging' was meant to be good or bad. The new Camille smiled. She already knew.

It wasn't just her newfound sense of confidence either — the same confidence that had made her apply to display her work in the gallery to begin with. It was the way that the man could not tear his eyes away from the pink stain in the center of the canvas. She was glad that this painting, above all her others, was the one garnering his attention. Undoubtedly, he would be thinking about it long after he had left. With any luck, he would not be the only one.

"I call it *Revenir*," she said.

"Revenir," he turned the word over in his mouth, chewing on it, considering its meaning. His eyes never left that stain.

She'd walked home in her ruined dress that night, one shoe missing, and she had laughed the entire way.

"I was taking French lessons," she said after a short pause in their exchange, and a quick scan of the room. It was important, she look engaged at any given moment, so she had to keep the conversation going. Still, it was not her desire to give too much away. The last thing she wanted was to spoil the mystique of her masterpiece. Less was so often more.

"You ought to keep taking them, if they inspire such work."

The comment left an unpleasant taste in her mouth and brought back unbidden memories. The ones from her life before.

Strange.

Since she'd woken up on the street, she had thought of John often. What she would do to him. What would make him tick. What would slide under his skin and nestle in to scratch at his veins. In detail, she'd imagined the toll the suspense must be taking on him. Not once had she taken stock of what exactly he had done to warrant her revenge.

Not once had she allowed herself to remember what had made her so vulnerable to the attack.

The glimpses into that old, before life were as unpleasant as they were fleeting.

She'd seen him differently, then. Not as something to be hated, but as someone precious to be revered. Handsome. Charming. Intelligent. The ghost of her desire sent shivers down her spine, when she had thought herself now untouchable.

"I don't believe my former tutor has anything left to teach me."

If her sentiment sounded as cold as it was intended, the critic did not seem to mind. To both her agitation and pride, he was more focused on her work than her conversation.

Her eyes flitted around the gallery once more, landing near the door.

"Speak of the devil."

John was the one who looked as though he'd been through something harrowing, not her. His suit was expensive, yes, but it didn't fit him half so well as the last time she'd seen him wear it. He'd lost weight. He'd lost sleep too, judging by the dark circles under his eyes.

He looked like hell, and she loved it.

She turned her body so that it faced the painting, inviting further conversation with the man beside her as she staked her spot at his side.

Easily enough, he took the hint that she wanted to keep talking.

"I see an almost impressionistic influence in your brush strokes here, is that right?"

"Partially," she admitted. "I spent the last couple years of my traditional training studying the impressionists. Lately, I've found I have more to say about the absence of light than its presence."

"Fascinating," he marveled.

"You flatter me."

He did, too. Though she knew her latest pieces were strong, worthy of praise, she did so long to hear it from another. She hungered for success more than she had before. The admiration of an esteemed member of their little art community did wonders to ease the small doubts she had about the conversation still ahead of her.

It had been so hard to find a dress that had covered all her scars to wear to her show. Now she felt as perfect and as whole as she'd intended to present herself.

The hairs on the back of her neck stood up as she felt her former lover approaching. She made no move to acknowledge it, rather urged the critic on with a small smile and nod.

"Do you mind if I ask...?" The words of his question trailed off, but his hand gestured to where his eyes had lingered; the pink stain. It was subtle, for a focal point, but the geometric, almost ragged nature of the blotch amidst such soft abstraction certainly succeeded in making its point.

John could not have chosen a better moment to arrive — better for her, at least. It was just as she'd been picturing all this time. She was smiling genuinely in front of her masterpiece while a prestigious member of the art world admired her creation. She'd been caught mid-conversation, mid success, even. It was almost too perfect.

"Camille," his low voice cracked in her ear.

She touched the critic gently on the arm in way of dismissal. "Pardon me for a moment, will you?"

"Of course, of course." He hesitated, but then finally broke away to take in her other pieces on display.

She turned to John with a wide smile.

His expression made her want to paint. It was all she had hoped for, and more. Her eyes glittered as she drank it in.

What had the last two months since their parting done to him? She didn't have to imagine much, since it had been a frequent fantasy of hers during that time.

He would have been anxious at first, scanning the news, waiting to hear the worst. It must have built up all the more as he reconciled what he knew to be true with the utter silence. He'd have been eaten away by the seeming lack of consequence.

Maybe, just maybe, there had been a moment of relief buried somewhere in there, where he truly believed he'd gotten away with it, hell, imagined it even.

Camille smiled at him politely, as if to ask what he wanted. She certainly didn't need anything from him; she'd already won.

"I... I didn't hear from you," he whispered.

She had not invited him, of course. That would have given away the game. It would have been contact. It would have been an admission that she still thought about him, even after what he had done.

She would have killed to see the look on his face when he'd heard about her show, however. Missing that had been the hardest thing.

"Did you want to hear from me?" She asked in her most innocent tone.

He didn't answer at first, but she rather suspected that the answer was no. Possibly, he'd been having nightmares lately of their next confrontation.

His lips curled up into a weak attempt at a smile. "It's just been awhile. I haven't seen you."

She had expected this. In lack of any external signs of anger, perhaps he thought things would somehow turn out okay for him. If she wasn't after him, if she didn't mean to tell anyone, perhaps he'd escape intact. Only she knew that she wouldn't have to. He was close to the edge, and would only require a little push from here.

"You're seeing me now," she whispered, letting her expression flicker momentarily to sinister.

He searched her eyes, pleading for an answer to his unasked questions. She nodded discretely to the painting behind her.

What little color he still possessed drained from him with a spark of recognition. He may not have comprehended all the nuances or the full meaning of the piece, but he remembered the street featured in the scene all too well. Staring at it, at her, it became impossible for him to shy away any longer from what they both knew.

She had been dead when he had left her.

Two months ago he had ended their lessons, and their brief affair, in a panicky, violent fashion. He'd dragged her out where no one would see and had let her life's blood becoming nothing more than a pink stain in the storm. She'd been cold and lifeless, and yet there she stood before him, living well.

It was too much. He wanted to scream and found that he had no voice. That deep, certain voice of his may never return.

She remembered then how enthralling she'd once found that voice, in that time before. Their early lessons especially, she'd been unable to get enough of it. There was one word that stuck out in her memory, one she'd always hear him saying.

Revenir.

It means "to come back."

The Six Suitors of Miss Lucy Westenra

♥

THERE WERE MANY MOST admirable qualities of Miss Lucy Westenra, who was as fair in countenance as she was in temperament. The young socialite was gentle and well-bred, coming from a fine and wealthy family. At nearly twenty years old, it was rather a wonder she remained unattached to any romantic partner.

It is said that when it rains it pours, however, and all of England seemed to grow wise to her presence all at once. So it happened that there was one most curious day when our young Miss Lucy found herself refusing no fewer than five propositions.

First, calling upon her at her parents' estate, was the honorable Dr. John Seward. He had been making such trips to her with increasing frequency, and had been spotted many a time already stealing glances at his companion. Still, she was surprised to come down to breakfast and find him already standing in the foyer at such an early hour.

"John?" She asked. "Is something the matter?"

"Nothing is the matter, Miss Lucy. It is only that I have a most urgent matter to discuss with you, and fear that it cannot wait any longer."

He led her, with her permission of course, into the gardens where he could walk and hide his nerves.

The doctor was not so forward as to take her hand, even when it was time to broach such a serious subject as the one he meant to address. She knew only of his intention to speak when he suddenly stopped walking.

"Miss Westenra," he said.

"John," she replied, for her gentle disposition meant such familiarities came easily to her.

"You are very dear to me," he begun his speech. "Though I have known you so little a time, I can tell already that my burdens grow lighter for your presence. As such, I cannot help but to believe my future woes would not seem disastrous at all were I afforded the chance to face them with you by my side. As such, I would humbly ask for your hand."

Miss Lucy was most startled, for though she was rather fond of the doctor, she had never considered him of any great romantic interest. He had excellent prospects, as a man through school already and overseeing the entire asylum by himself.

But there had to be more to life than schooling and excellent prospects — hadn't there?

All the same, she contemplated his offer; it being her first proposal after all. No one else had ever offered marriage, and a woman her age really ought to settle down as soon as possible. She feared she would not receive another chance.

Careful consideration deemed him too serious of a fellow, for she simply could not wed a man who did not make her laugh.

"I am sorry, John," she said, and not without a hint of true sorrow in her chest. "I do not think I can wed you."

"Is there another?" John asked.

"There is," she told him.

She thought of another man she hoped to marry, and how joyous she would look at his side on their wedding day.

"Then you have my apologies," he told her before stalking off, eager to leave the embarrassment behind him.

Miss Lucy returned to her private chambers too contemplative to even break her fast.

Her next meal also was interrupted by a gentleman caller, and before she could even have a single bite. Mr. Quincy P. Morris came along and asked her if he might steal her away for a leisurely walk along the grounds. At this, her spirits lifted considerably, for she thought him to be an absolute delight of a man, one who could always seem to tell when her spirits needed lifting.

Only his intentions did not seem so altruistic on this particular occasion, and he did not show the young doctor's restraint when it came to touching her. He plainly — and rather boldly, it could be said — lay it all bare before her after grasping her one hand in both of his.

"Miss Lucy," he said. "I know I ain't good enough to regulate the fixin's of your little shoes, but I guess if you wait till you find a man that is you will go join them seven young women with the lamps when you quit. Won't you just hitch up alongside of me and let us go down the road together, driving in double harness?"

Well, it was the strangest proposal Miss Lucy had ever heard of! The slang had her in fits, giggling even as she declined.

"I know not of hitching," she told the jolly American suitor at her side. "But I should tell you before you think of riding off anywhere with me that there is another."

He tipped his hat to her, but did not depart without first stealing a kiss. She was relieved — and yet also somewhat disappointed, at how lightly he took her answer.

Though they could have shared many laughs together, she was still a young thing, and easily influenced by the presentation of a man. She pictured how handsome a husband she might claim for herself, and how pretty she might look standing next to him. With two proposals under her belt already for the day, she had some hopes that a third, more dashing man might yet be on the horizon.

Miss Lucy retired to her chambers with no lunch, and ample time to consider the peculiarity of the morning.

Tea-time rolled around and brought her just the visitor she had hoped to see. His name was Arthur Holmwood, and he was truly the most handsome man she had ever laid her green eyes upon.

"My darling," he said with a voice warm enough to melt harder hearts than hers. "There is no better time on this Earth than the hours I am fortunate enough to spend by your side. Should you allow me, I would like to keep your company as much as possible, and to that end I would name you my wife before another man wises up and attempts to do the same."

Oh, how our dear Miss Lucy had longed to hear such a thing from his lips.

Yet, the thought of spending the night with him — indeed every night with him for the rest of her life — was a notion that paled in comparison to all the excitement she'd already had that day. It would be unwise, a madness even, to refuse the object of her affection, but her curiosity demanded that she see what else might be in store for her.

"Might I have the night?" She asked this man, whose attention she had so craved just earlier that same day. He looked taken aback, as

KILL YOUR DARLINGS

well he might, for she had given him every reason to believe he already possessed her favor.

"The night?" He questioned.

"Yes," she replied. "To think it over."

"I must say I am surprised. Perhaps I have been mistaken in my belief that you already share my affections?"

He looked so wounded that it was all she could do to hide her smile. Never before had she dreamed that she might have such power over a man that she could wound him so with only her words. That feeling was more intoxicating than all three of the proposals combined.

She put her hand over top of his most gently.

"Mr. Holmwood," she said, rubbing salt in the wound, for she had not addressed him so formally since that first occasion where they had met. "I hope you can forgive me my hesitation in the matter. I fear it has been quite the long day."

"What has happened?"

"Before you arrived," she told him, watching his expression closely, "there were two other fine matches who made the same request of me."

Oh! How the jealousy writ on his face filled her with such devious delight. She had never seen Arthur half so flustered as he looked, standing there before her.

"What did you tell them?" He lamented.

"That I had eyes for another," she teased.

"And was I not that other, Lucy?"

The absolute anguish in his eyes was marvelous.

Suddenly Miss Lucy wondered why she had to ever marry at all, when such deep emotions could be evoked by the refusals. She tried to shake such foolishness from her head, as she knew she would not remain nineteen and pretty forever, no matter how fun the day had been.

"It was," she confessed, and she tried her best to look remorseful. "But the weight of not one, but two such conversations can now be felt upon my heart most heavily. I was so anxious that you would not come."

"But I have come, Lucy."

"Yes," she said. She knew this was the part where she ought accept his most generous offer. "You have come, Arthur, and I am most grateful for it. Truly I am, only..."

"Only what?"

There was such decadent torment in him as she feigned indecision. She wished she could make it last a lifetime. "Only I do not feel quite myself at present."

It was true enough that Miss Lucy was feeling quite queer in her cravings.

"Shall we call John?" Arthur asked, being quite close to Dr. Seward. "Surely if you are ill —"

"We needn't call John," Lucy told him quickly. The idea of making both men more fully miserable in her presence, perhaps competing for her affection, it took her breath away. Such indulgences would have to be spread out, lest they prove more exciting to her than she could bear. "I just need to rest for a while. I should rather have this conversation once I have had the time to collect myself, and might give you my full attention. I shall take this night to rest, if that is alright with you?"

She posed it as a question, knowing there would be no courteous way to refuse such an earnestly presented request.

Being a gentleman, Arthur consented, albeit begrudgingly. "I shall return to you tomorrow," he said, "and spend this night praying you greet me with good news."

"I am sure I shall," Lucy said, though she was sure of no such thing.

No sooner had Arthur left than she found herself quite a wreck. She did not miss him so much, but she missed his attention. When she tried to picture herself in all her wedding finery, she could not picture a man at the altar beside her in front of whom she might express herself truly. She needed a partner who would understand her feelings, even these strange ones that she could hardly understand herself.

By the time she met her good friend, Mina Murray, for dinner, she was ravenous — though she found herself only picking at the meal, for it was not food she craved.

"I do not know how to describe it, Mina," she told her confidant, from whom she had never hidden a secret in all her life. "Arthur has been all I have hoped for these past many weeks and yet..."

"Yet when given the chance to have everything, you found it no longer tempted you?" Her best friend finished for her, as though she had just plucked the thoughts straight from her mind.

"You must think me mad," Lucy groaned.

"On the contrary." Mina reached across the table to take her hand. Often she had made this gesture, but never before had it carried so much weight. Though it might have passed for a sisterly motion between friends, the look in Mina's eyes was far from familial. "I know exactly how you feel."

Miss Lucy felt her cheeks redden. "You do not mean to say that you had such doubts about Johnathon?"

"I mean to say, Lucy, that I harbor such doubts about Johnathon even now."

Lucy had to drink deep of her wine to combat the dryness that suddenly filled her mouth. "You two seem so happy."

"In many ways, he is all I could hope for. He is a kind man, patient, and easy enough to look upon... only..."

Lucy resonated with that hesitation in her friend's voice. "Only...?"

"Only he does not see me, Lucy. Not truly. He does not understand me the way a husband, and I should hope a lover, ought see me — in both body and soul." There was another moment of silence as Mina worked up the courage to meet Miss Lucy's eyes. "The way that you see me."

"Mina..."

Lucy trailed off, finding she was entirely at a loss for words.

"Would it not be better to spend your life with someone who knew your heart so intimately? Someone, perhaps, that had grown up beside you, and known you all your life?"

The urgency of the confession could be felt as a spark between them, though the language of it remained most vague. The fire stirred something most sinful in our dear Miss Lucy.

"I could see how such a match might have its perks," she admitted softly.

This was dangerously close to what she had wanted already, a life in service to no man, but only her womanly whims.

"I am not as daring as you, Lucy, nor has God blessed me with your fine features. But I have savored every moment of your trust and you know I want for nothing but to see your smile."

Miss Lucy thought about it. She contemplated such forbidden thoughts longer than a proper lady of her standing ought to have entertained such a scandalous notion. Mina was the person who knew her best, after all, and Lucy could almost imagine the two of them wearing the white bridal gowns together.

Of all the offers put before her thus far, Mina's embrace had sounded sweetest. Even the taboo nature of such a life, however, did not reach levels equal to the desire for true danger which had been unearthed that day in our gentle lady.

"Mina, you are more than a friend to me. I consider you a sister, and—"

"I would die for you, Lucy. Truly I would." There were tears in the other woman's eyes. "You need not say the rest. This was a madness in me, a fleeting fancy is all. We need not speak of this further, or again."

So they did not speak of it. Lucy spent the rest of the dinner swirling her wine and wondering how those sweet tears might taste upon her tongue.

When the two friends parted ways, Miss Lucy did not return to her parents' home. Her mind and body were both too restless to entertain the notion of sleep.

She wandered out into the city.

It was a most strange experience. She had spent her life in England, and knew this particular area most intimately by the light of day, only to see how different it looked after sunset. The streets emptied out and took on a most sinister quality. Homeless children ducked around corners, and she fancied she could hear cries echoing from each alley. Every shadow seemed to stare at her. She wondered as she walked if the world had always been so full of darkness, and how she could have been so blind to it before.

Lucy sat down on a bench, not stopping to consider her poor parents, and how they must be fretting over her. They had sheltered her with so many comforts she had not ever stopped to think about the cold, hungry children. The uncertainty of an orphan's future put her own doubts quite to shame.

A man sat down on the bench beside her, so suddenly and silently it was as if he had solidified from the mist itself. There was no shine in his pitch black eyes.

She searched his face and found herself at once transfixed by his dark visage. He said not a single word to her, but she'd grown accustomed enough that day to promises to recognize just what he was offering when his teeth slid into her slender neck.

For that moment, she became one with the stranger.

There were glimpses through the pain of what her life might look like as his eternal bride. There was finery, and wealth, a castle, and more danger than she could ever wish — especially as she knew his influence was spreading. He was older than the others that had come before him, yet time would never steal so much as another day from his features.

The visions were so tempting that she almost succumbed once she had gotten that first taste of immortality. Once more she pictured herself in all white, gorgeous, and ready to claim all that she had ever desired.

But it was not the darkness in the fantasy beside her, nor was it this darkness made flesh that sat beside her while she thought, having pulled away to watch her most expectantly. In the image she had curated of what her heart desired most, she stood quite alone.

"I am sorry," she said dreamily, for the thrall of the night creature had not worn off entirely. "But there is a sixth suitor who beckons me."

The stranger said nothing, but nearly watched another monster bloom into the world. She had, after all, the strength to pursue her own desires above even what he could offer, which made her an absolutely singular woman of her time.

She knew she had chosen well. She had means, humor, the looks, the understanding, and now the danger to be all she had ever wanted in a partner, and could carve her own way through the city.

So Miss Lucy Westenra had sat on the bench, but it was The Bloofer Lady in all her glory that rose. And it was just as beautiful as she had dreamed.

Story Notes

As I mentioned in my introduction, I'm very attached to and proud of all of these stories. I think they stand well enough on their own that reading through the story notes is entirely optional. (If they did not stand on their own, I would not be releasing them.) However, if you are interested in my process, the feedback, or even the rejections associated with the pieces, I have taken the liberty of including that information below.

My Salt, His Wounds

This story truly embodies the spirit of this collection. It was the first story I wrote for myself with the intention of using abstract elements. Even though I hadn't written it for a specific call, it was shortlisted by many publishers for a variety of anthologies, magazines, and even a couple fiction podcasts before being sent back home to me. I like to think that maybe it was destined to kick off this collection, in much the same way that it kicked off my very weird phase of writing.

d3t0x

This is possibly the most frustrating entry of the book. I had this idea for a dystopian, sci-fi horror novella about an app that would let you sign up to give microdonations to causes you cared about whenever one of your contacts did something you didn't agree with politically. I sat down to start writing it, and basically wrote this story. I felt like a fucking *genius* when I hit my core theme in just ten pages. I worked with it, whittled it down, and thought this might be the best short story I'd ever written. My beta readers loved this one. My friends were really enthusiastic about it. Publishers on the other hand just weren't interested. It did make one short list before I was eventually told that it "didn't make the final cut." This is the only piece in the collection that I never received personalized feedback or constructive criticism for at any stage of the writing or submission process.

Maybe it really should have been a novella. Maybe some day it will be, because I had a ton of fun writing this story and I stand by the concept. All I know is that this one turned out exactly how I wanted, and it's wild to me that it was still available for this collection.

The Grass Red and the Trees Dark

This is one of the more personal pieces. They're all very personal in that they all represent something different I wanted to try, and capture a very specific moment of my writing. But this one feels like part of my blood. I was obsessed with stories when I was a kid, but there were very few tales that felt like a part of my culture, to the extent that I feel comfortable as an adult adapting them through a horror lens. Me being very Irish, however, I feel like fairies fall into that realm.

I also feel it represents some of my preferences as a reader (and biggest vices as a writer.) It's a slow-burn, right up until it isn't. While it was shortlisted, the length was a common critique I received with the rejections for this one. I cut it down when and where I could, but the truth is that as a reader, I like indulgent, detail-oriented writing that moves at a slower pace. I also love the fever pitch of ending. While I have learned, generally, to be more discerning of where to employ generous details, this story still embodies some of my best work in vivid prose.

Castaway

Another commonality in this collection is toying with the idea of what is and is not real. If I were forced to only write one subgenre for the rest of my life, it would be psychological horror, because I love pushing the limits of that concept. I had a lot of stories that I was writing around this time where I was trying to learn how to play with the audience's perceptions. This story was one where I really wanted to play with the reader by choosing to write from the perspective of the imagined party. It's one thing to tell the story of a dying man who imagines his own rescue, with staff that tries to trick him into drinking ocean water and sealing his fate. It felt far more innovative to me to tell that same story from the perspective of one of the people he has imagined.

Even though the piece came out more abstract than I had hoped initially, it truly has cemented something in my style. It broke a habit of needing to overexplain things in every piece that I do. From the surreal element that this evokes, down to the island setting, I think "Castaway" served as the seeds for my upcoming novella, *The Desert Island Game,* which is probably the strangest thing I've written to date.

L'Arabesque

This is probably the most indulgent tale in a collection that is all indulgence. It's long. It's a little gross. It's very strange. There is more French than anyone asked for or probably wanted. These all sound like criticisms, but they're also exactly what I look for in my horror. They're mostly the reasons I love the movie *X* so damn much. I want bloody ballerinas being gross overtop a French soundtrack in my horror. I'm not sure I've ever written a story that is more indicative of my own tastes in this genre.

Enlightenment

This story feels the least like my own writing when I read it back. There are a lot of stylistic choices I recognize as mine, and it has a very bleak ending that appeals to my sensibilities, but there's a certain technical edge that is somewhat uncharacteristic. Ana felt like a very ambitious character for me to write, and there was a lot of research that went into this story (as opposed to my usual system of just writing on topics I've already voluntarily done the research for.) This one took me out of my comfort zone in a way the other stories did not.

This is the only story in *Kill Your Darlings* that actually received an acceptance letter prior to me querying this collection. I wrote it specifically for a charity anthology where it was not accepted, but where I was encouraged to submit to a different anthology that the press was working on. It was accepted there and scheduled to be published before the press owner was involved in a scandal and shut everything down.

I was grateful not to have my work associated with the press at the time, but also, I was devastated that this piece wouldn't see the light of day. I am so glad that now it's finally getting its second chance to be out in the world.

Imaginary, But Very Real

This one surprised me a lot. I was in a writing slump and wrote this as a prompt response. I ended up submitting it to a couple places just because the deadlines were creeping up, and I didn't have anything better. I didn't love it at the time. I was so surprised when it was shortlisted, and the positive feedback in the rejection letter was actually the thing that got me out of that particular slump.

I've cleaned the story up a lot since it was rejected, but I still think it's a testament to the fact that some rejection letters can do more good than an acceptance.

You'll Just Be Nothing

While we're on the topic of rejection letters, "You'll Just Be Nothing" is one of my craziest, and most encouraging rejection stories of all time. I would call bullshit on this if another writer of around my (nonexistent) fame level told me this story. But I swear, it's 100% true.

I submitted a different story to a very prestigious indie press. They rejected it, rightly, and I didn't even question the decision. They emailed me about a year later to invite me personally to submit to their upcoming theme anthology, on the grounds that I had submitted to them before. I was 90% sure that this was a form letter that they sent to all the writers who had submitted work before, because it seemed totally impossible that they had remembered me, specifically.

I was on death's door at the time, and not supposed to be working. I was so afraid that on the off chance that it wasn't a formality and they genuinely wanted *me* submitting work to them, that I'd never forgive myself if I didn't have something ready. So, I slogged my way through writing this with a fever and a cough and I put all of my energy into making it as presentable as I could. I sent it in and then I saw the list of very prestigious writers who had been invited (not just invited to submit, but invited to *be in* the anthology). There were some big names, and it actually made me a little sick, because I knew my writing was just not of that caliber. There was no world where it was possible that I was going to be in that anthology with those heroes of the indie horror world.

I was beyond discouraged at that point because I'd put everything into this piece at a huge personal cost, and I was pretty sure I was never going to hear from this press again. I had convinced myself that the invitation to submit was a mistake and I'd nearly killed myself just for the chance at a form letter rejection. You know, because the story is here, that it *did* get rejected. But first, it made it to the last round of considerations, which seemed impossible. And when the rejection came it was a personal note from the editor, along with the feedback from the first readers who made the decision not to pass it through.

The feedback was that they wanted more, and one of them said that they wanted it to be a whole book.

I have never come to close to sitting down and starting a novel on the spot as I was when I read that. I was in the middle of editing my debut at the time, not to mention writing a different novella that is scheduled for release next year, or I think I would have done it. I quit submitting this one because I fully intended to adapt it just based off of that letter. I almost didn't include it in this collection. Much like "d3t0x", I can absolutely see myself revisiting these characters somewhere down the line.

Ultimately, I decided that right now, I have enough books in my brain trying to claw their way out, that I didn't need to turn this into a full, new project. I told the story that I wanted to tell for the time being. I just wanted to share this little moment between two characters, with this high concept power that is never fully confirmed, and this moral dilemma that doesn't reach it's conclusion.

But who knows. Maybe some day it will.

In the meantime, I'm really grateful to have it here with the other stories. While I'm putting together a collection in the spirit of gorgeous rejection letters, I think it's completely fitting this piece be included.

Until He Starves

I have always liked playing with elemental horror, but realized at some point that I didn't have any air/wind pieces. "Until He Starves" was my attempt to rectify that, though it morphed early on into more of a mythological horror piece. I try (generally) not to play too much with Greek mythology because it's something that gets adapted so often. Over the last several years I've only been interested in seeking retellings from Greek voices in that space. But I grew up hearing a lot of Greek myths and sometimes the urge to dabble in those stories is just stronger than I can resist.

Revenge Body

I don't know what to say, other than I just had a lot of fun writing this one. I wrote it for a specific anthology that just was not interested in it at all. I shopped it around with some body horror anthologies after that, but honestly, I like writing body horror too much not to do new stories for all those calls. The biggest feedback that I got for this one was that it could have been a lot bloodier. From a body horror perspective, I think that's true, but as a revenge piece with some fun wordplay, I like the balance just fine.

Ramen of Regret

I (sort of) wrote this for a very specific call. Unfortunately, the idea itself was inspired by their list of things that they were not interested in receiving at that time. It wasn't a hard limit, so I sent it anyway and apologized in my cover letter for doing the one thing I wasn't supposed to do. The rejection letter that inevitably came was very sweet. They told me they liked it well enough that they considered it anyway, but it just wasn't what they were interested in at that time. I thought that was totally fair, and very kind of them to say. Outside of that one call I honestly just had no idea where the hell to place this thing, so that was my only time submitting it.

Twelve Hour Lifespan

There were two calls that I really wanted to submit to, but I was running out of time. One was a bug anthology, and the other was an apocalyptic anthology. So I wrote this one, strange story with the intention to submit it to both, before ultimately deciding it didn't fit either project particularly well. I did send it to some weird horror anthologies and the consensus, overall, was that the story was "too bleak."

In context, I think the story was just too bleak for the anthologies in question, but it took me back to my first attempts at publication. I started out writing depressing little zombie stories, and "too bleak" was a criticism that I got *all the time.* It felt, in a strange way, endearing to be receiving those sorts of notes again, like I had come full circle in my writing journey.

Not Like Lettie

Folk horror!

As I was learning about subgenres and testing my range, I found that I avoided folk horror because it was so daunting. In my mind, it just felt very research intensive, and easy to mess up. "Not Like Lettie" was a breakthrough moment, where I realized I could invent my own rituals and cultures and strange religious ceremonies that could backfire for participants. They did not need to be researched as thoroughly or rooted completely in fact. Carving out these sections of the world and thinking about how isolated societies might have hypothetically evolved under terrible conditions is a fascinating experiment in fiction writing. Approaching it from that angle, as I did for the first time with this piece, takes some of the pressure off, and I think offers many elements I love most about world-building.

Out of all the pieces in this collection, this was probably the one I got the most constructive criticism for, despite it being an "almost" at several outlets. Some publishers thought it was too long already, while others felt that it should have been a lot longer. Subsequently, I have a version of this story that is about half the length, and one that is considerably longer. I also have an outline for a novella-length version that follows Judah's journey from the death of his father all the way through his escape of the island, with this story serving as more of a climax than a stand-alone tale. Since beta readers and publishers and friends couldn't agree on how long this piece should be, I ultimately chose to include the version of the story *I* liked best. This was my second or third draft and I personally like the balance of it. It alludes to all of Judah's history without becoming bogged down by him as a presence. He's an outsider, a witness, and I feel he serves that purpose without the audience needing to know him better than they do.

While this is as long as *this* story needs to be, in my opinion, I have taken the tools to create other, fictionalized pockets of terrible society. My piece "First Blood" deals with similar rites of passage and questions tradition in a more personalized character arc, and it's roughly three times the length of "Not Like Lettie." You can read it in Ruth Anna Evans' upcoming *Dark Blooms* anthology. I would, some day, like to do longer, stranger, folk horror writing.

Revenir

I said that "L'Arabesque" might be the most on brand story for me, but this would be its strongest rival. It's also a little French, there's some word play, there are scary resurrection themes, and it's about revenge. These are all my favorite elements and tropes all rolled up into a single piece that felt very natural for me, both in style and length.

The Six Suitors of Miss Lucy Westenra

This is the one story in the collection that is really just not original at all, but all the dialogue and characters I used are from Bram Stoker's *Dracula*, which is in the public domain. I put it last, because I think of it as sort of a bonus story? A fun exploration into something different than what I'm usually up to.

While some of stories in the collection may one day be longer projects, this one was actually cut out of a longer project I was working on. I might, or might not be, gearing up to release a modern retelling of *Dracula* (that I may or may not have already purchased cover art for.) In deciding the new dynamics and foundation for the story, I decided to reimagine some of the motivations and archetypes.

Particularly I wanted to play with Lucy Westenra. She was such a symbol of purity and loss in the original text, and I have seen modern and feminist takes of the character where she uses this deep morality to fight the corruption that she succumbed to in the original. I thought it would be much more interesting (and perhaps spoilers for my upcoming book) to see what it would be like if Lucy was *not* a force of good. What if Lucy chose evil? For herself? Because she wanted to?

It's a big theme for the project, and even though I ultimately chose a different style and timeline for the work in question, this was my first foray into making that shift for her as a character. It's an exploration into her temptations, how those could be reinterpreted, and what might drive a wholesome young woman to want to become, well, The Bloofer Lady.

Acknowledgements

There are always so, so many people to thank in the backs of novellas. With a short story collection, it is literally more individual people than I could list. This collection is brought to you not just by me, not just by PsychoToxin, but by every first reader, beta reader, slush reader, editor, critique partner, writing group member and supportive friend who believed in one or more of these stories.

I also want to thank the following people who believed not just in a single story, but in the collection as a whole: Ruth Anna Evans, Tasha Reynolds and Angel from Voices From the Mausoleum. You are all such beautiful and supportive friends generally that I don't know what I would do without you, but all three of you specifically told me that it was a good "next step" in my career to release these stories into the wild. You were absolutely right.

Adam Hulse also deserves a shout-out here. I'd been working on this collection for maybe a week when I found out about his collection entitled *Not A Good Fit At This Time,* which he was already about to release and which had a very similar premise. I was feeling very insecure about attempting this, and reached out to ask him about a hundred questions about how he put his collection together. He could have accused me of stealing his idea, or brushed me off, but instead he was so nice and gave me some of the best advice about how to curate this thing. Adam, thank you so, so much.

And finally, a big thanks to Christopher Pelton. I love every time I get to work with PsychoToxin, but this project in particular has been a dream publication from start to finish. I hope that in the coming years I can cement my reputation as a writer who always has something weird ready to go in the chamber on short notice.

About the Author

Cat Voleur is a writer of dark fiction and host of two podcasts, Slasher Radio and The Nic F'n Woo Cage Cast. When she is not creating or consuming morbid content, you can most likely find her with her army of rescued felines, pursuing her passion for fictional languages. She is featured here with her supervisor, Atticus.

Also By

Revenge Arc
All of These People Are Going to Die 4: Heck House
Puppet Shark: The Novelization
The Desert Island Game (Coming Soon)

Printed in Great Britain
by Amazon